THE WALL

AND OTHER STORIES

THE WALL

AND OTHER STORIES

JUREK BECKER

INTRODUCTION BY CHRISTINE BECKER

Arcade Publishing • New York

First Edition

Arcade Publishing books may be purchased in bulk at special discounts for
sales promotion, corporate gifts, fund-raising, or educational purposes. Special
editions can also be created to specifications. For details, contact
the Special Sales Department, Arcade Publishing, 307 West 36th Street, 11th
Floor, New York, NY 10018 or arcade@skyhorsepublishing.com.

Arcade Publishing® is a registered trademark of Skyhorse Publishing, Inc.®, a
Delaware corporation.

Visit our website at www.arcadepub.com.

10 9 8 7 6 5 4 3 2 1

Library of Congress Cataloging-in-Publication Data
Becker, Jurek, 1937–1997.
  [Short stories. Selections. English]
  The wall and other stories / Jurek Becker; introduction by Christine Becker.
— First edition.
    pages cm
  ISBN 978-1-62872-325-0 (hardback)
  1. Becker, Jurek, 1937–1997—Translations into English. I. Title.
PT2662.E294A2 2014
833'.914—dc23   2013049434

Printed in the United States of America

Contents

Introduction

by Christine Becker

In the late eighties, four hundred fifty photographs of the Lodz Ghetto were discovered and a plan for an exhibition was put into motion. Jurek received copies of the pictures and was asked to write about them. He examined them with feelings of horror, excitement, and hope, knowing they could depict his parents or even himself. And he wrote "The Invisible City," which begins with the bare facts about himself, presented in his typical sober and ironic manner: "When I was two years old I came to this ghetto. At age five, I left it again, headed for the camp. I don't remember a thing. This is what people told me, this is what is in my papers, and this was, therefore, my childhood. Sometimes I think: What a shame that something else is not written there." These first sentences already provide insight into the lifelong burden that became the topic of this text—and which characterized all his works. As a personal testimony and the only nonfiction text, we have placed the essay at the end of this collection.

The title story, "The Wall," relates the experiences of a young boy in the ghetto. When the child and his parents are interned in a provisional camp, which is separated from the ghetto by a wall, the story takes the form of an adventure. Together with his friends, the boy hatches a plan that he keeps secret from his parents and eventually carries out: the wall is to be surmounted.

Jurek, at the age of forty, wrote the story consistently from the perspective of the child. This allowed him to provide a momentary view of the ghetto and of life in the camp while at the same time refraining from projecting contemporary values on the situation. Without a doubt, "The Wall" is the work of fiction in which Jurek most engages with his childhood. It is hard to believe that memory is supposed not to have played any role.

Jurek's first novel, *Jacob the Liar*, which brought him international acclaim, had already been interpreted as a story of recollection. He insisted, however, that it was purely inspired by what his father had told him. In the plot of *Jacob the Liar*, another child plays an important role. After her parents are deported, Jacob takes Lina into his care.

Jacob supplies an entire ghetto with news from a radio that circumstances force him to invent. He merely heard one real news report, by chance, but— once circulated among the ghetto inhabitants—the report inspires such hope that henceforth Jacob feels obliged to lie. He begins to claim that he owns a radio.

Eventually, Lina wants to listen to Jacob's radio too. Jacob gives in and, sheltering behind a wall, presents the little girl with the broadcast of a fairy tale. This is the "Tale of the Sick Princess," a fairy tale embedded within the novel. Here, just as he would later do in "The Wall,"

Jurek grants the influence of childish behavior: the children make child-appropriate demands, which seem inappropriate in light of the given circumstances but, by the same token, lend some normality to their own existence. The assertion of normality in turn gives people dignity within an undignified situation and frees them from the only role they are so often assigned retroactively, which is that of the victim. The fairy tale can be read as another contribution to the topic of childhood in the ghetto, and so is included in our collection.

"The Most Popular Family Story," as the title suggests, addresses the issue of storytelling itself, storytelling in general as well as the specific practice of telling stories as a part of family tradition. The narrator is a member of the younger generation who tries to reconstruct a funny story that, in years before his time, was traditionally told at family gatherings. At the beginning of the story, Jurek addresses the narrator's doubts about his enterprise, and later he switches off between the embedded and framing narratives. Jurek himself liked to recite the story at public readings, more frequently so than any other text. I myself heard it countless times and could not wait to see how time and again his audience interrupted him with laughter. It was his intention to make us laugh, and only in one, incomplete sentence does the story's background shine through: the loss of the family through displacement and murder.

After a childhood spent in the ghetto and concentration camps, Jurek was left with only his father to tell him about the past. His mother had died shortly after the Red Army had liberated the camp. But his father, like so many survivors, was rarely prepared to provide information. His energy was consumed by trying to make a life for himself in postwar Berlin. He had settled in the eastern part of the city. It was here that Jurek first went to school at the age of nine, and he later became a citizen of the socialist East German state.

Thus, in 1961, Jurek bore witness to the erection of the Berlin Wall, which was to become a portion of the barrier—unconquerable to those in the East— separating the two German states. Visible every day, the wall created East and West Berlin, each subject to the laws of their respective countries, with different economic conditions and different currencies.

In 1977, after prolonged and fierce conflict with the authorities and with their approval, Jurek left East Berlin. He traveled to the United States for the first time, was writer-in-residence at Oberlin College in Ohio, and later settled in West Berlin. He had retained his East German passport and could routinely cross the border in both directions. Naturally, the life situation of the inhabitants of both parts of the city became the subject of his prose.

In the short story "The Suspect," the protagonist, from whose perspective the story is narrated, finds himself surprisingly and unfairly subject to surveillance by the state authorities. Without being explicitly mentioned, the story can be assumed to take place in East Berlin—the German Democratic Republic had quickly gained the

reputation of being a police state. The nameless protagonist is portrayed as loyal to the state and uncritical; for
this reason the surveillance he is under appears to him as
a mistake. To disperse the suspicions against him, "the
suspect" undergoes a self-evaluation and begins to cease
all behaviors that could be construed as suspicious. At
the end of his efforts—at the end of the story—he again
makes a surprising discovery. We experience the narrator
to be assiduous and yet surprisingly dispassionate, and
eventually the process of surveillance and self-regulation
is not only menacing but at times also funny.

"Romeo" tells the story of a young migrant worker
who lives and works in West Berlin and of a young
woman from East Berlin. His high rent, low wages, and
the favorable exchange rate between the two German
currencies entice him to try to quintuple his money on
the illegal exchange market. He searches for and finds a
young woman in East Berlin who can provide accommo-
dation. Both characters behave in a pragmatic manner,
yet it remains unclear whether their connection is bound
purely by its purpose. The director Andreas Dresen, one
of the most renowned directors of contemporary German
film, saw a film plot in this and wrote the author: "It is
notable that among the cool calculation there is also a
degree of warmth. There is this spark of hope for humane
action, even under adverse circumstances that demand
otherwise—and that usually dominate us." Dresen's
movie was made in the year the Berlin Wall fell, and thus
represents an era that was soon to end.

The story "The Wall" was also turned into a film in the early nineties. For the project, Jurek collaborated with director Frank Beyer, who had already received an Academy Award nomination for his screen adaptation of *Jacob the Liar*. And then it finally happened: Jurek was describing the furnishings of the small room in the ghetto where the little boy and his parents live. And suddenly everything had its place: table, cupboard, a stool with a tub on it. . . . Excitedly, he got up from his desk and stood before me. "Since I have no memories—how could I know? How would I know exactly what the room looked like?" he asked. It appears that, for once, he succeeded in unlocking at least part of his childhood.

In the nineties, the years after the reunification of the two German states, Jurek had retreated from the commotion of Berlin to the countryside. Once more, an unexpected political development had relegated him from actor to observer. He had come to Germany involuntarily, had only learned the language in which he wrote at the age of nine, and according to him had never felt fully German. It is to this late and attentive acquisition of language, however, that Jurek owed his literary language, which was later lauded as especially clear and precise. And being an outsider allowed him to take the step back that enables us to see the whole. Both may help explain why, in his prose, Jurek dared to engage with the unimaginable and unspeakable—and to suspend the widespread impulse to close one's eyes and ears.

THE WALL

AND OTHER STORIES

The Wall

Here I am, at a time when we Jews are quietly minding our own business and our neighbor is called Olmo who spends half the day quarreling with his wife, and if you have nothing better to do you can stand behind the door and hear every word. And the street still has its houses, in each of which something has happened to me. I'm not allowed to leave it, the street—Father has strictly forbidden me. Often I don't believe his reason for this, but sometimes I do: that there is a boundary, an invisible one, beyond which children are snatched away. No one knows where it runs, that's the sneaky part. It seems to be constantly changing, and before you know it you've crossed it. Only in our own street, it seems, are children relatively safe, safest of all outside their own house. My friends, with whom I discuss this enormous problem, are of two opinions. The know-it-alls laugh, but there are others who have already heard about it too.

I ask: "What'll happen to me if they catch me?"

Father replies: "It's better for you not to know."

I say: "No, tell me—what will happen to me?" He merely makes a vague gesture and refuses to talk to me any more. Once I say: "Who is it anyway who snatches away the children?"

He asks: "Why do you have to know that too?"

I say: "It's the German soldiers."

He asks: "The Germans, our own police—what's the difference if they catch you?"

I say: "But there's a boy who plays with us every day who lives many streets away."

He asks me: "Is your father a liar?"

I'm five years old and can't keep still. The words tumble out of my mouth. I can't keep it shut, I've tried. The words push against my cheeks from the inside, multiplying at a fantastic rate and hurting my mouth until I have to open it. "What a child!" says my Mother, who no longer has a face, only a voice. "Just listen to that child, that crazy child."

What happened must have been strange, unheard of, otherwise it wouldn't be worth telling. For all I know I may have killed Mr. Tenzer, the shopkeeper. I'll never find out. He lives in our street and wears a little black cap and has a little white beard. He is a tiny little man. When the weather is cold or wet you can go to his place. He tells stories. The toughest kids sit silently in front of him, not saying a word, never opening their mouths, perfectly quiet, even though later they make their jokes. But he never lets more than four come in at one time. I am his favorite: it makes me feel good believing that. Once when he picked me up and put me on top of the cupboard—he proved to be very strong. We were all surprised.

Father says: "What kind of person would put a child on top of a cupboard? And anyway, why are you always hanging around old Tenzer? He must have a screw loose."

I say: "You have a screw loose." He swings his arm back, but I run away, and when I return later he's forgotten all about it. Father often swings his arm back, but he never hits me.

One day I've quarreled with everyone and go over to Tenzer's place. I've never been alone with him before. When he opens the door and sees only me outside he's surprised and says: "Such a small gathering today?" He is busy doing his laundry, but he doesn't send me away. I am allowed to watch. He washes differently from my mother, who always splashes water all over the room. He handles the underpants and shirts gently, trying not to make even more holes, and sometimes he sighs over an especially big hole. He holds a shirt high above the bowl, and while it drips he tells me: "It's thirty years old. Do you know what thirty years means for a shirt?"

I look around the room; there's not much to look at. There is only one thing that I've never noticed before. Behind the high headboard of the bed, on the floor beside the window, stands a pot. A large cloth hangs in front to hide it. I would never have made the discovery if I hadn't been lying on the floor and looking in that very direction out of boredom. I make a little detour over to the thing. I push aside the cloth, which would hide it from someone twice my size. In the pot there is a green plant, a strange one that pricks sharply as soon as you touch it. "What are you doing back there?" shouts Mr. Tenzer after hearing me cry out. There is a drop of blood on my forefinger—I show him my thick blood. I stick my finger in my mouth and suck it; then I see tears in his eyes and am more scared than ever.

I ask: "What did I do?"

"Nothing," he says, "nothing at all, it's my fault." He explains how the plant functions and how many animals would have eaten it if it weren't for the prickles. He says: "You're not to tell anybody about it."

I say: "Of course I won't."

He says: "You know that no one's allowed to have a plant?"

I say: "Of course I know that."

He says: "You know what happens to anyone who ignores a rule?"

I say: "Of course."

He asks me: "Well, what do they do to him?" I don't answer. I just look at him because he's about to tell me. We look at each other for a while, then Tenzer picks a piece of washing out of the bowl and wrings it out violently. He says: "That's what they do to him." Of course I tell the story to millions of people, not to my parents but all my friends.

I pay another visit to Mr. Tenzer because ever since that day he has allowed me to play with his plant as if we were brother and sister. The door is opened by an old woman, so fearfully ugly that anyone in my place would have been terrified. She asks in a nasty voice: "What do you want here?" I know that Tenzer has always been alone and wouldn't have dreamed of letting such a person into the house, so the fact that she is in his home alarms me even more than her appearance. I run away from the witch and pay no attention to the curse she calls out after me. The street hardly sees me—I just fly along it. I ask my Mother where Mr. Tenzer is. She starts to cry. Only a moment ago she had been embroidering the cloth to which she belongs. I ask: "Where is he? Tell me!"

But I have to wait for Father to tell me when he comes home that evening: "They've taken him away."

By this time I'm no longer surprised, hours have passed since my question, and many times they have taken someone away who was suddenly no longer there. I ask: "Whatever did he do?"

Father says: "He was *meshugge*."

I ask: "What did he really do?"

Father rolls up his eyes and says to Mother: "You tell him, if he really wants to know." And at last she says, though very softly: "He had a flowering plant. Just imagine, they found a flowering plant in his room." It is rather quiet. I am suffering because I mustn't say that the plant and I are friends. Tears drip from my Mother's eyes onto her cloth. Never before has she had a good word to say for Tenzer.

Father cuts his chunk off the loaf as he does every evening after work. I am the real sufferer but no one takes any notice of me. Father says: "I've said it all along, he has a screw loose. To be taken away for the sake of a flower—of all the ridiculous reasons!"

My Mother has stopped crying but says: "Perhaps he loved that flower very much. Perhaps it reminded him of someone, how do we know?"

Father with his bread says loudly: "That's no reason to put a pot of flowers in one's room. If someone insists on living dangerously he can plant tomatoes in a pot. You can remember a person a thousand times better with tomatoes."

I can't contain myself any longer. I don't like my father very much at this moment. I shout: "It wasn't a flower, it was a cactus!" Then I run outside and remember nothing more.

Father wakes me in the middle of the night; the curtain in front of my bed has been pulled aside. He says:

"Come along, my son." He bends over me and strokes me. My mother is also fully dressed. There is movement in the house, footsteps and clattering sounds through the walls. He lifts me out of the bed and sets me on my feet. To keep me from falling over with sleepiness, he supports my back with his hand. It's a good thing he's not hurrying the least bit. My Mother brings me my shirt, but I sit down on the bucket that is our toilet. The moon rests on the crossbar of the window; suddenly there are two bulging carryalls in the room. If you look long enough at the moon its face doesn't stay still: it winks at you. Then my Mother pulls my shirt down over my head. "Come along, my son," says Father. They both try to think of what they might have forgotten; Father finds a pack of cards and stuffs it in my bag. I also have something to take along: I place the cloth ball my Mother made for me beside the bags, but I am told there's no more room. Then we walk down the pitch-dark stairs, across the whispering courtyard, out onto the street.

Many people are there already, but none of my friends. "Where are the others?" I ask Father.

He lets go of my Mother's arm and says: "It's only our side of the street. Don't ask what it all means, those are the orders." This is a disaster, since my friends all live on the other side.

I ask: "When are we coming back?" They stroke my head again but explain nothing. Then we tramp off in response to a command given by someone I can't see. The way becomes more boring with every step; we must be crossing the invisible boundary ten times over, but when you're given orders of course the ban is lifted.

A small section of the ghetto—and this has nothing to do with memory, it's the truth—a small section of the ghetto is like a camp. A few long barrack-like brick huts standing at random are surrounded by a wall. It's not so terribly high; from day to day its height seems to me to vary. Certainly, if one man stood on the shoulders of another he could look over it. And if you stand back far enough you can see broken glass glinting on the top. But why have a camp in the middle of the ghetto, which is camp enough, you wonder? To which I can reply, though no one explained it to me at the time: people are assembled in this camp before being taken to a different one, or to a place where there is more need for them than in the ghetto. In other words: the idea is to be in readiness in the camp. Is it a good sign to be here, is it a bad one? This is debated day and night in the long brick huts. I'm sick of hearing it.

The three of us are allotted one bed, a hard affair made of wood. Though it is a bit wider than my former one, we are miserably cramped. There are also some empty beds in the hut. Right after the first night I lie down on one of them and announce that from now on this is where I'm going to sleep. Father shakes his head. I shake my head in reply and ask for his reasons, at which he swings his arm back again. I have to yield—it is a victory of unreason. We experiment with various positions: myself on the left, then on the right, then with my head between my parents' feet. "That gives us the most room," says Father, but my Mother is afraid that one of the four feet might hurt me. "Sometimes a person kicks out violently while dreaming. You don't realize it, but you do."

Father can't deny this. "All the same, it's a pity," he says. I end up lying in the middle, not consulted, and must promise to move as little as possible.

Every morning there is "inspection"—that's the first word I learn in the foreign language. We line up in a long row outside the hut. It all has to be done very quickly because a German is already standing there waiting. The tips of our toes mustn't be too far forward or too far back. Father straightens me out a bit. The first person in the row has to call out "One," then we number off to the end of the row. The numbers roll along and pass over my head. My Mother calls out her number, then Father calls first his and then mine, and already it's the next person's turn. This annoys me—I ask: "Why can't I call out my number myself?"

Father answers: "Because you don't know how to count."

"Then you can just whisper my number to me," I say, "and I'll call it out."

He says: "First of all there's no time for that, and second—we're not allowed to whisper."

I say: "Why don't we stand at the same spot every morning? That way we would always have the same number and I could learn it."

He says: "Listen, my son, this is not a game."

There are two in my row who aren't much older than I am, one of them calls out his own number, the other one's number is called by his father. I ask one of them: "How old are you?" He spits past my head and walks away. He must come from the upper end of our street—I rarely got that far. After the numbering the German shouts: "Dismissed!" That's an inspection.

By the second day I'm already bored to death. There are a few smaller kids around, but when I approach them their leader tells me: "Beat it, but *pronto*." They all look at me angrily, those idiots, just because their leader wants to show off with that word. I ask my Mother what *pronto* means, she doesn't know. I say: "It must mean something like quickly."

Father says: "Who cares?"

The camp is dead, and I can't bring it to life. I start to cry, but it doesn't help. In one corner of the camp I find a little grass. I mustn't go too far away, my Mother says; Father says; "Where can he possibly go to here?" I discover the gate, the only place where there is movement—sometimes a German comes in, sometimes one goes out. A soldier who is a sentry walks up and down until he sees me standing there. He raises his chin quickly. I can't say why I have so little fear of him. I take a few steps back, but when he starts walking up and down again I retrace my steps. Once more he moves his head like that—once more I do him the favor—then he ignores me.

That afternoon a different soldier is standing at the gate. He calls out something that sounds dangerous. I go into a hut that is not ours. Though I'm afraid, there's nothing else for me to do. The same beds are there, and there's a stench that isn't like anything I've ever smelled. I see a rat running by—it gets away from me—I crawl on my hands and knees and can't find its hiding place. Someone grabs me by the scruff of the neck. He asks me: "What are you doing here?" He has one blind eye.

I say: "I'm not doing anything."

He stands with me in such a way that the others can see us. Then he says: "Tell me the truth."

I repeat: "I am not doing anything. I'm just looking."

But he says in a loud voice: "He wanted to steal, the little bastard, but I caught him."

I shout: "That's not true!"

He says: "It's true all right! I've been watching him all morning. He's been waiting for hours for a chance."

One of them asks: "What are you going to do with him?"

The liar says: "Shall I beat him up?"

One man says: "It would be better to boil him."

I scream: "I wasn't going to steal, really I wasn't!"

I can't get free of his grip, and the liar squeezes harder and harder. Luckily, someone calls out: "Let him go, he's the kid of someone I know." But he holds onto me a bit longer and tells me not to let him catch me again. I don't tell Father anything about it; most likely he would punish the disgusting fellow—but then I'd have to stay in our own hut. It's not worth it.

Next day all is well again: early in the morning the other side of the street moves into the camp. I've hardly taken five steps outside when someone sounding like Julian calls me and hides. I needn't look very far. He's around the next corner, pressing himself against the wall and waiting for me to find him. Julian is my good friend. We haven't seen each other for a long time, maybe a week. His father was a doctor, that's why he's always well dressed, even now.

He says: "Well, I'll be damned!"

I say: "Julian." I show him around the camp—there's not much to show—his hut is the farthest away from ours. We look for a spot that from now on is to be our special place: in the end he picks it, even though he has been here only a few minutes and I have probably been here for as long as a week.

He asks: "D'you know Itzek is here too?"

He takes me over to Itzek's hut—Itzek is my good friend too. He is sitting on the bed and has to stay with his parents, so he can't be glad about me. We ask his father: "May he at least go outside with us for a bit?"

His father says: "No chance." But when Itzek begins to cry he gets permission from his mother, who is normally very strict. We show Itzek our special place; we sit down on the stones. The wonderful thing about Itzek is his turnip watch—I look at his trouser pocket where it is always ticking away. Twice so far I've been allowed to hold it to my ear, and once he let me wind it, after I had won a bet. His grandfather gave it to him because he loved him, and told him to keep it well hidden or else it would get pinched by the first thief to come along. Julian also has something wonderful, a wonderfully beautiful girlfriend. No one has ever seen her except him. She has fair hair and green eyes and loves him madly. Once he told us that they sometimes kiss. We didn't believe him so he showed us how she purses her lips. Only I own nothing wonderful. Father has a flashlight with a dynamo that has a handle you have to squeeze to make it light up. But if one day he can't find it we all know who'll be suspected first.

I say to Itzek: "Show me your watch." But his rotten parents found it and swapped it for potatoes. Julian still has his girlfriend. Itzek is crying over the loss of his watch. I don't make fun of him. I would try to comfort him if I weren't too shy. Julian says: "Stop crying, kid." So Itzek runs away, and Julian says: "Never mind him." And the splendid turnip watch has been swapped for potatoes—it defies comprehension. I tell Julian what a day in this camp is like so he won't expect too much. Until Itzek comes back Julian tells me about his girlfriend—her name is Marianka.

Since I left our street, nothing much has happened there. Only Muntek the cobbler has committed suicide. Whenever we sat on his steps he used to come out of his dirty shop and kick us. Now he's dead. It's a funny feeling because only the other day he was still alive.

I ask: "How did he do it?"

Julian says he slashed his wrists with glass and bled to death. Itzek, on the other hand, who lived three houses nearer to the cobbler than Julian, knows that Muntek plunged his cobbler's knife into his heart and twisted it three times.

Julian says: "I never heard such nonsense!"

They argue for a while until I say: "What's the difference?" But the story also has a sad ending because Itzek's mother had left a pair of shoes with Muntek for repair. When she heard of his death she hurried over there, but the shoes were gone—the shop had already been stripped.

Still sitting down, Julian pees between me and Itzek in a beautiful arc. He can do that better than anybody. Then he has a plan and makes a solemn face. He wants us to put our heads together. He whispers: "We have to go back to our street—at night would be best." Julian has never made such a crazy suggestion before.

Itzek asks him: "Why?"

Julian turns his eyes toward me, indicating that I should explain to this idiot, but I'm at a loss myself.

Julian says: "The whole street is empty now, right?"

We answer: "Yes."

He asks: "And what about the houses?"

We answer: "They're empty too now."

"The houses aren't empty at all," he says, and all of a sudden he knows something we don't know.

We ask: "Why aren't the houses empty?"

He says: "Because they're full, stupid." He despises us for a little while, then he has to explain, otherwise we would leave. So: the street was emptied, house by house, but as we know better than anybody, the people weren't allowed to take much with them, at most half their possessions. The other half is still inside the houses—by Julian's estimate there must be great piles of stuff still lying there. He tells us, for example, that he hadn't been able to take along his big toy motorcar because his fool of a mother had trampled on it and instead had given him a bag full of underwear to carry. I remember my gray cloth ball. Only Itzek didn't have to leave anything behind—he had nothing.

"You'll never get over the wall," I say. Julian throws a stone at the wall—the stone passes so close to my head I can feel the wind.

He asks me: "Over that one?"

I say: "Yes, over that one."

He asks: "Why not?"

15

I say: "The Germans are watching night and day."

Julian looks around with wide eyes, then says: "Where do you see any Germans here? Besides, they sleep at night. Didn't you hear what I said? That we have to try during the night?"

Itzek says: "He's got wax in his ears."

I say: "Anyway, the wall's much too high."

Itzek says to his friend Julian: "You can tell how scared he is."

All Julian says is: "We'll have to look for a good place." Julian says to me: "Coward."

We look for a place and of course Julian is right, there is one, where metal struts have been put in like steps. "What did I tell you?" says Julian. My heart beats fast because now I have to go with them or be a coward. There is another advantage to the place: it is far away from the camp entrance and so it is also far from the sentry. Though there is another sentry who walks around and eventually passes every spot, most of the time he is in his little German guardhouse, sitting and smoking or lying down asleep.

Julian says: "I will tell you again, the Germans all sleep at night."

I ask: "How do you know?"

He answers: "Everybody knows that."

And Itzek points at me and says: "Only he doesn't."

"Shall we go tonight?" Julian asks, looking at me.

I think how easy it would be to agree to everything now, and later simply not show up. I look at the struts and test the bottom one with my hand.

16

I say: "The Germans must be crazy."

"So what do you say?" Julian asks me again.

I say: "Why don't you ask him too?"

Julian asks Itzek: "Shall we go tonight?"

Itzek is silent for a moment, then says: "Tomorrow night would be better."

"Why wait until tomorrow night?"

Itzek says: "One shouldn't rush matters." This view is familiar from his father, a lawyer by profession (whatever that means).

My preparations begin that evening. If ever I am to succeed in getting out of bed at night unnoticed, I mustn't sleep between my parents—I must sleep at the edge. I start coughing until my Father wants to know what's the matter. My Mother places her hand on my forehead. The coughing goes on and on. I can see them whispering together. As I lie down I say: "I can't get any air in the middle. Don't worry, I won't fall out." And I cough so violently that I really do have to gasp for air so that they have to give me a place at the side.

Every night someone shouts: "Lights out!" then the light goes out; for a short while whispering continues. The elves fly in the dark—they are a secret that must never be spoken about. Once when I wanted to talk about elves with my Mother she merely put her fingers to her lips, shook her head, and said nothing. The roof of the hut opens up to the elves, the walls bend down to the ground, but you don't see anything—you just feel the waft of air. They float in and out, just as they please. Sometimes one of them brushes you with her veil or with the wind. Sometimes she even says something to you, but always in elfin language, which no human can understand; besides, elves speak incredibly softly. Everything about them is more delicate, more gentle, than with humans. They don't come every night, but not that seldom either—then there is a hidden, joyful movement in the air until you fall asleep, and probably even longer. At the first hint of light they vanish.

Tonight I intend to practice getting up, I've told myself: if I manage once to get out of bed without waking them, I'll also manage when it really matters. Only I must be sure they've fallen asleep.

Normally, Father falls asleep so quickly that he is already snoring before the elves arrive. Sometimes I poke him deliberately in the ribs, and it doesn't disturb him. But tonight of all nights they whisper together and lie with their arms around each other like children and kiss, as if they hadn't had all day to do that. I'm stuck—they've never kissed like that before in the hut.

I hear Father whisper: "Why are you crying?" Then I feel sleepy—I believe the first elves are already there. I roll my eyes to drive off my tiredness.

I hear my mother whisper: "He's stopped coughing, do you hear?" Then Father wakes me and says: "Come along now, inspection won't wait for you."

My Mother says to Father: "Let him be, he hasn't had enough sleep." Such a disaster won't happen to me again, I swear, even if I have to prop open my eyelids with matchsticks. So tonight I'll have to leave the bed and the hut with no rehearsal; but the good thing is that I now know how easy it is to fall asleep against one's will.

Father nudges me in the row. I look up and hear him say under his breath: "Twenty-five!" Though my mind is already on the coming night, my heart beats faster, now that I have a chance to show what I can do. The numbers come rushing along—the eyes of the German facing us always stay with the number. I'm scared; Father cannot know what kind of a moment he has chosen. I have to press my lips together not to call out too early, then I shout "Twenty-five!" It must have been exactly the right moment, after the woman ahead of me and before Father—the numbers roll away from me without a hitch. It's a good feeling.

After inspection Father says: "You did that splendidly. Only next time don't shout so loud." I promise. He picks me up in his arms—that's not nice in front of all those people.

We meet—Julian, myself, and Itzek—and wait for the coming night. Julian has noticed that at our chosen place there is no glass on the wall, which is very lucky. Itzek says he noticed that too.

Julian says: "I needn't bother to go to our old room. I'm going somewhere else right away. Are you going to your rooms?" I consider whether our room is worthwhile: the cloth ball is still there, maybe the flashlight too—it hasn't shown up yet in the camp.

Itzek says: "Honestly now, who's scared?"

"Not me," says Julian.

"Not me either," says Itzek.

"Not me either," I say. I ask Julian whether he wouldn't like to visit his girlfriend when we're outside.

He answers: "Not at night, silly."

A cold wind drives us away; only Julian knows where to go. He knows of an empty hut; we run there. Though I don't like to admit it, Julian is the leader among us. There is no door. We step into the dark room, which contains nothing; only some two-tiered bunks pushed against the walls such as I've never seen before. Itzek climbs around on them and jumps from one to the other, like a cat, and Julian looks at me as if everything here belonged to him. Then someone says: "Clear out, and I mean now!" Itzek is so terrified that he falls off a bunk, picks himself up, and runs outside. Julian has already disappeared. I am left standing alone in the middle of the room. The voice, which sounds both tired yet as if coming from a strong person, says: "What's the matter with you?" I stand there out of sheer curiosity; besides, Julian will see which of us is a coward.

I say: "With me?" Then something white emerges slowly from a bunk, far back in the mountain of bunks. I've seen enough. I rush out into the open where Julian and Itzek stand at a safe distance, waiting and perhaps glad, perhaps disappointed, that I have emerged unscathed from the danger. I say: "Phew, you should've seen what I saw!" But they don't want to hear my story. It's barely raining now.

We decide to meet at our special place and then go over to the wall together. Julian asks, why not meet at the wall right away, and I have a reason: if one of us is late, it wouldn't be such a good idea to wait for him at the wall.

After we have agreed, Julian says: "We'd better meet at the wall."

Without giving it much thought I ask: "When are we going to meet anyway?"

We think about this for a bit, then Julian looks at me angrily as if with my question I had actually created the problem. He always needs to blame someone and says to Itzek: "If you weren't so stupid and still had your watch, there'd be no problem."

Not one of us can think of a sign in the night to tell the time by. Until Itzek says: "Lights Out is the same time everywhere, isn't it?" That's the best idea yet, even Julian can't deny that, "Lights Out" could be the kind of sign we need. "Right after Lights Out," says Itzek, "then one more hour, then everybody will be asleep, then we can meet."

"And how long is an hour?" asks Julian, but he has no better suggestion. We agree on the length of an hour: it is the time that even the last person in the hut needs to fall asleep, and a bit longer. We place our hands one on top of the other and are sworn conspirators and separate until nighttime.

Then I am back with my parents sitting on the bed. My Mother gets up from her sewing and says that I am wet through. She takes off my shirt and dries my head. Many people are walking around in the hut, their hands clasped behind them: one of them is Father. Someone sings a song about the cherries a pretty lass is always eating, about the bright dresses she is always wearing, and about the little tune she is always singing.

For the first time in my life I can hardly wait for night. The fear has gone. That's to say, it's really still there but it is not as great as the anticipation I feel. If only I don't oversleep, I think, if only I don't oversleep again, I mustn't oversleep.

I tell my Mother: "I'm tired." It is still afternoon. She lays her hand on my forehead, then she calls Father. "Strange—he's tired and wants to sleep."

Father says: "Are you surprised if someone runs around all day and gets tired?" My Mother gives him an exasperated look. He says: "Let him lie down and sleep, if he wants to and can," then he starts walking around again.

I lie down. My Mother covers me up. She asks whether anything hurts—she presses a few places. I say impatiently: "Nothing hurts."

She says: "Don't be cheeky." She leaves her hand on my body under the coverlet. I don't mind—it feels quite pleasant. As time goes by I really do feel sleepy, what with the rain beating on the roof, the people walking around in slow circles, and her hand on my stomach. I think about what I would like to find in the empty houses in the night—it mustn't be too heavy as I will have to carry it, nor too big; I keep an open mind— just that the word "marvelous" keeps going through my head. I'm sure I shall find something to make people stare and ask: Where in the world did you get *that*? Then I shall smile and keep my secret to myself, and they will all rack their brains and be envious. I feel I'll soon be asleep—there's always a humming in one's ears just before sleep. There's no chance of my oversleeping, I think, no matter how tired I may be: every night someone shouts "Lights out!" loud enough to wake a bear. I am quite clever.

I sleep, then I'm awake again. It's almost time to go to bed. I am given my piece of bread and half an onion. I am a bit surprised that no one seems to notice what remarkable things are going on. Only my Mother insists that something's wrong with me; her hands keep fluttering over my forehead, and she reminds Father about my coughing. I am about to jump up and show her how well I am, but I remember just in time what a mistake that would be. I mustn't be well yet—I must go on coughing—otherwise they'll put me back between them for the night.

"There you see?" says my Mother.

She wants to fetch Professor Engländer, the famous doctor from the next hut, but Father says: "Go ahead, fetch him. He'll come and examine him, and if next time it's something really serious he won't come again."

A voice calls: "Lights out!" One more hour, I think in alarm. Itzek is lying there now, Julian's lying there now. I think, for each of them, one more hour. I'm afraid my parents may be able to feel how I'm trembling inside, but they are already at their kissing and whispering again. I never felt so wide awake in my life. Over and beyond the disturbance beside me I am aware of every single thing happening in the hut: the whispering in the next bed, the first snore, a groan issuing not from sleep but from misery, the second snore, the concert of snores, through a gap in the wall a light from the sky. I notice the rain has stopped—somewhere drops are still falling onto the ground, but no longer onto the roof. Two beds further along there's a very old woman who talks in her sleep. Sometimes it has woken me up. I am waiting for her to start again. Father says one can be a different person in one's sleep.

She is silent. Instead someone is crying—that's not so bad—crying makes a person tired and soon drop off to sleep. Then I hear a snore that delights me because it is my Mother's. The sound is very soft and irregular, with little hesitations as if there were an obstacle in its path. None of the elves has put in an appearance yet. Perhaps the rain is keeping them away tonight. A good part of the hour has passed. I don't want to be the first at our meeting place. The hour will be over, I decide, when Father is asleep too. I sit up and dangle my legs over the side of the bed. If he asks me what's the matter it means he's not asleep. But he doesn't. Itzek is also sitting on his bed, that's a help. Julian's heart is also beating fast now. The crying has stopped, and for a long time there have been no more whisperings. So my hour must be up.

I stand beside the bed and nothing happens. Twice that morning I found my way to the door with my eyes shut—to make up for the lack of rehearsal during the night—and I didn't bump into anything. All I did was step on the toes of an old man who was in my way, and he gave me a piece of his mind. I pick up my shoes. The hour is over. I take one step, then another. The floor creaks a little. During the day you don't hear that. The darkness is so black that it makes no difference whether your eyes are open or shut. My steps quicken, but suddenly everything stops. I almost fall over with shock because someone screams. It's that awful old woman.

I don't budge till she is quiet again; what will happen if she wakes my parents, and then: "Where's our child?" But they go on sleeping because the woman's screams are part of the night. My legs find the corner by themselves, then I see a gray shimmer from the door—light from the night. The last steps are recklessly fast because it suddenly occurs to me: what if the doors are locked at night! But the door opens with wonderful ease and closes quickly—at last, I'm outside in the camp! I sit down, put on my shoes, and could kick myself: I've forgotten my trousers. When I go to bed I always keep my shirt on, taking off only my trousers—that's my Mother's system here: the trousers are folded up as a pillow on the bed so no one will steal them. Now I have to climb over the wall in my shirt and underpants. Itzek and Julian will make fun of me.

I can't find the moon. Yesterday I asked Julian: "What'll they do to us if they catch us?"

He replied: "They won't catch us." I found that very reassuring.

On the ground are puddles. In one of them I find the moon. Of course I stop at every corner and take no risks. I think: even if Father wakes up now, it won't do him any good.

Beyond the last corner I find Julian crouching by the wall. Of course he laughs and points at me. I sit down beside him on the ground. He is still enjoying the joke.

I ask: "Isn't Itzek here yet?"

He says: "Look around for yourself, stupid."

The bottom strut is so low that I can hold it as I sit there; it wobbles a bit. "Maybe he fell asleep," I say. Julian says nothing—he seems very serious now that he's stopped laughing. Never before have I been so aware of his superiority. I ask: "How long are we going to wait?"

He says: "Shut up." I imagine Itzek's horror when he wakes up in the morning and it's all over. But now there's no time for pity. I'm waiting for Julian's orders and begin to be afraid of the wall. It is much higher than during the day. It grows with every passing moment. When a crow caws overhead, Julian stands up; perhaps the bird's call was the signal he was waiting for.

He says: "Your Itzek is a coward."

Later, after we have returned with our booty, I shall be just as great a hero as Julian. It'll make no difference then who gives the orders now and who obeys. But Julian is silent for so long that I am afraid something may have gone wrong.

I ask: "D'you want to postpone it?"

He says: "Rubbish." I admit there was also a bit of hope in my question, but now I know we're going to leave the camp tonight.

"What are we waiting for?"

He says: "Nothing." He pushes me aside because I am in his way. He tests the first strut, the second, and the third. He can't reach the fourth from the ground. He steps onto the first strut and is now high enough to touch the fourth. Then jumps down again on the ground. He says: "You go first."

I ask: "Why me?"

He says: "Because I say so," and I feel how right he is.

Even so I ask: "Can't we draw lots?"

"No," he says impatiently, "get on with it, or I'll go alone."

That's the highest proof that Julian isn't scared like me; he gives me a little shove, to help me pull myself together. True, I can still think of a few questions I'd like to ask him; but if Julian means it and goes without me I'll look like a fool. I step up to the wall. He says: "You must grab the third one and step onto the first."

He pushes from below to make it look as if I couldn't have managed without his help. I stand on the bottom strut and no longer feel scared of the wall, only of the height. It is a consoling thought that I shall have conquered the wall when Julian still has to face it. It's like a ladder for giants. First take a big step, then grab hold of a higher strut—not much effort needed for that. On my right is the cool wall, on my left down below Julian stays farther and farther behind. He has turned his face up to the sky and is watching me.

He asks: "How's it going?"

For the first time in my life I despise him, and from my height I say: "Don't make so much noise." I won't let him know how easy it is; it was only fear that made him send me first. Suddenly, the top of the wall is level with my eyes.

I see a street. I see dark houses, the damp cobblestones on the square. Nothing moves. The Germans really are asleep.

Softly, he calls: "What can you see?"

I call back excitedly: "Way down there is a cart drawn by horses. I think they're white."

He calls out in surprise: "You're lying!"

I say: "Now it's turned a corner." I lean my arms on top of the wall. There is a bit of broken glass lying there. They are small pieces—you can't see each one. I grope along the wall with my hands. The largest piece can be broken off, and I use it to scrape away the other splinters.

"What are you doing?" Julian asks from below.

I carefully brush off the glass with my sleeve and blow. Then I roll over onto the wall. The fear starts up again—most of all I'm afraid of the fear. I have to get my knees under my stomach, that's the hardest part. For a moment I put my knee on glass. Of course I mustn't scream. I find a better place for my knee. It must be bleeding now; and Julian, the idiot, calls out: "What's keeping you?"

I have to turn myself around. I'm desperately afraid of losing my balance. If Julian says one more thing I'll spit on his head. Then, after turning around, I see him standing down there and for the first time realize how high up I am. Once again I lie down on my stomach. My legs are already outside. I can't worry about little pains. I let myself down as far as my arms will stretch. My feet find no support because there are no struts here. I hang there and can't pull myself up again.

I hear Julian calling: "What's going on? Say something!"

I close my eyes and picture the wall from below, how small it seems when you walk around in the camp. So what can happen? I'll fall down and hurt myself a bit. I've fallen down thousands of times. I'll get up again and wipe my hands, while Julian will still have to face the climb. What happens if he doesn't come? I get cold shivers at the thought—I'm hanging here and Julian disappears and goes to bed. I can't very well go alone into the houses; after all it was Julian's idea from the beginning. I call: "Julian, are you there?" Then I fly through the air: though nothing has been decided yet, the edge of the wall has detached itself from my hands. The ground is a long time coming. I fall slowly—the wall scraping along my stomach the whole steep way down—finally landing on my head too. I lie there comfortably on my back, keeping my eyes shut for a bit before calmly looking at the sky, which is exactly above me. Then I see Julian's face on the top of the wall. He's a good fellow, and he's got guts too.

He calls: "Where are you?"

Now I must move. I have two pains to cope with, one on my right hip, the other in my head. I say: "Here, Julian." I feel giddy too. I must move to one side so he doesn't make matters worse by landing on my head. I think: But I've made it.

Julian has a different method. He sits on the wall. He slides forward; he seems to be hurrying; he supports himself left and right; his arms soon look like wings on him. No, he's not a coward. He flies to the ground, landing beside me on his back. He gets up much faster than I did. Since I am behind him I walk around him, but he turns so that I can't see his face and he moves off a few steps. I want to see him and grasp his shoulder, but he pushes me away because he's crying. Even so he's got guts.

My headache is sometimes a little one, sometimes a big one. My hip hurts at every step. I ask: "Are your hands bleeding too?" As if this possibility had occurred to him for the first time, Julian looks at his hands, turns them toward the moon. They aren't bleeding. To comfort him I show him mine.

He says: "What on earth did you do, you donkey?"
I say: "The glass."
He says: "The whole idea is not to touch that."

I am shivering—how many jackets does a thief need at night? We are now people in a story, Julian walking ahead; he asks: "Are you still there?" That means he can't hear me—I slink along as stealthily as any expert. With each step I get more used to my hip, whereas my headache gets worse. Everything is fine as long as I don't turn my head. Somewhere a dog barks; it is a long way away and has nothing to do with us.

I say: "Why don't we go into this house?"

We go up to the next house, but the front door is locked. We try every door, but it's the same with all of them. I cry a little, from my headache and the cold too; Julian doesn't laugh. He tugs at my sleeve and says: "Come." That makes me feel better. He says: "D'you know what I think?" And when I shake my head and so cause myself new pain, he says: "I think there are people still living here. That's why the houses are locked up. Only our street is empty.' I stop outside a window and want to find out whether Julian is right. I stand on tiptoe to see if there are people sleeping in the room. A devil's face looks out at me—only the pane of glass is between us. I run away, hip and all, so that Julian doesn't catch up with me until the next street corner.

I say: "There was a devil behind the window."

Julian says: "There are people living there, stupid."

He finds our street. I hardly recognize it in the dark. We walk past a fence where two loose boards seem familiar to me. I push one of them with my finger and am right. I could show many a trick in our street. I ask Julian why he doesn't simply take the next house;

yet I know he is afraid it might be locked up too. He says: "I know what I'm doing."

Then I feel fine because my head feels better. We would have been inside a house long ago if Julian felt as cold as I do. I think: I hope he won't feel warm for too long. Some day or other I'll be the leader, then I'll wear warm clothes. He asks: "Are you still there?" We go past my house—he can think only of his own; without him I could walk in if I wanted to. I think of Father's flashlight. I must be tired. We waste no words over the workshop of dead Muntek, the cobbler; in my day, anyway, he was alive and used to chase us. I have never felt so cold in my street—the wind blows around my bare legs—but Julian is the first to sneeze. He stands outside his house and can't get through the door. He rattles it a bit and kicks it a bit, but the door stays shut.

I say: "Don't make such a racket!"

He answers: "Shut up."

Since it is a long way to my house, I go to the next one, and that's open. I call Julian; we're very close to our fortune. The house has three floors. We start at the top because Julian wants it that way. On the landing it's black, a door opens, a dark-gray hole. My heart pounds because I don't know whether Julian has opened the door or a stranger, until Julian says: "What are you waiting for?" In the room there is a confusion of things: overturned chairs, a table, an open cupboard in which our hands find nothing.

I ask: "What's that stink here?"

Julian says: "You stink."

I sit down on a broken bed. Julian goes to the window and opens it. It gets lighter. He leans far out and asks: "D'you know where our camp is?"

I go over to him and say: "No."

He shuts the window again and says: "I do." That's Julian for you. On the way back to the door we stumble against a bucket, where the stink comes from.

All the rooms in the house are empty in the same way. In one there is an object that is much too heavy to take along. Julian says: "That's a sewing machine." In one we find a box half full of coal—what use is coal in the camp? In one the handle falls off the door. I pick it up and decide to take it along—it'll do for a start. Julian takes the handle away from me and replaces it. In the next house, in the very first room, Julian finds something. He examines it and soon calls out: "Wow, they're binoculars!" I have never heard this word. He says: "Come here and look through them." I go over to him at the window, he holds his discovery up to my face, and sure enough you can see things in it that no one can see with ordinary eyes, although it's night. Julian shows how I have to turn the little wheel to make the pictures fuzzy or clear, but I can't see anything anyway because suddenly there are tears in my eyes. I give him back his binoculars. What rotten luck that he should be the one to find them.

In the next room Julian comes to me and says: "We must go back."

I say: "I'm not going before I find something too." He repeats that I must hurry, as if it were a question of skill whether I find something or not. He stays with me in each room, as long as I like. He opens every window and looks at everything with his damn binoculars.

I feel I would be content with less and less, but there is nothing there. Julian says: "We must go. Or d'you want them to find out everything?" I say there is just one more room I want to go into, that's where the cloth ball is lying under the bed, then we'll run back to the camp. "All right," says Julian; since the binoculars he's a generous friend. While we walk along the street I have no answer to the question of what will happen if my house, of all the houses, should happen to be locked. Julian sees it long before I do, through his contraption, and says: "The door's open." There is no ball under the bed. I crawl into every corner. When we left the room it was here, no doubt about that, so someone came later and stole the ball. Now the whole thing hasn't been worth it.

Julian asks: "What's wrong?" because I am sitting on the bed crying. He puts his hand on my shoulder, though he could easily be grinning. He's a pretty good friend. Now he should ask whether I want his binoculars; of course I wouldn't accept them, but it would help a lot. Then I remember Father's flashlight. It hasn't shown up in the camp so far; maybe it'll show up here, if the cloth-ball thief hasn't found it. I don't know where Father kept it hidden. I don't think it had any fixed place; sometimes it lay on the table, sometimes somewhere else.

I get up and ask Julian: "If you had a flashlight as big as your fist, where would you hide it?"

He looks around three times, then asks: "Are you sure it's here?"

I say: "It must be here."

Julian puts down his binoculars on our table and begins to search; I like that but then again I don't like it. I hurriedly start searching; I must find the flashlight before he does. There are a few places I know that he doesn't—a hole in the floor, a little hollow under the windowsill, a loose board in the top of the wardrobe. My knowledge yields me nothing. I crawl on my stomach across the room, I climb on the chair: no flashlight. If Julian says once more that we have to leave, we'll have to leave. For the last time I crawl under the bed, and I hear him say: "D'you mean this one?" He is quite calm. He has placed the flashlight on the table without waiting for any thanks.

I ask: "Where did you find it?"

He says: "In the drawer." He says it like someone who can't understand that I almost went out of my mind over such a ridiculous object. He takes his important binoculars and goes to the door. Perhaps

I would never have thought of the drawer: you don't need to crawl on your stomach to reach it; you don't have to climb on a chair; not even the ball thief had that much sense.

Back in the camp I'll make the light shine; just now Julian is impatient. I hurry after him to the stairs, yet I'm the one who knows every step of the way here. "Thanks, Julian," I say or think. Suddenly, I feel sorry for Itzek. Julian forbids me to try out my flashlight in the street. I do as he says. I pay no attention to where we're going. I just follow him. I don't feel cold yet. I have to hold the flashlight in my hand because of course, having forgotten my trousers, I don't have pockets.

I ask: "D'you remember the way?"

"You can go by yourself if you like," says Julian, which means he knows the way. I've no idea why he is angry. I want to be nice to him.

I say: "If you need the flashlight, you can borrow it any time."

He says: "I don't need your flashlight." I believe he's just as eager as I am to be home again—that puts him in a bad mood; he dreads facing the wall again just as much as I do and having to climb it and jump down into the depths.

I say: "If the Germans are all asleep, we don't need to climb. Why don't we simply walk through the gate?"

"Because it's locked, stupid," says Julian.

It gets colder as we walk along. Of course, Julian finds the camp and since I've never doubted it I feel no relief. He even finds our spot. He whispers: "Oh no, d'you know what's wrong?"

I whisper: "What?"

"The iron struts," he whispers back, "there aren't any on this side."

I'd like to have had a bright idea too and whisper: "We have to go around the camp, somewhere there must be these things."

"But there's glass all along the top of the wall, except at this place," whispers Julian.

I look at my hands, which I had forgotten, and my knee. I whisper: "If we find another place, we'll take a stone and first break up the glass." I realize how good my idea is, for now Julian says nothing and looks for a stone. He puts the stone in his trouser pocket and sets off as leader; if we should find struts on this side of the wall, it'll be me who has saved us.

While walking ahead Julian says: "Stop playing with your stupid flashlight or I'll take it away from you." He's always bossiest when he's right; I would be a better leader if I were the leader. We have to make a detour, a big detour away from the wall and past the camp entrance, where there's not a soul to be seen. That's how Julian wants it. He takes away my flashlight, though I've done nothing with it. For safety's sake, I don't resist; a leader must think of everything and needn't explain everything. We sneak across the street, which leads straight back to the camp gate. There's still no one there to see us. We get back to the wall. Julian returns my flashlight, which is what I expected. We walk and walk and find no struts.

I say: "Julian, there won't be any."

"I know that perfectly well," he says, but keeps walking.

Then I ask: "How much longer are we going to walk?" His answer is to stop, sit down, and lean his back against the wall. I sit down too and don't ask. I look at Julian and see something terrible: he is crying. Now for the first time we're stuck. He is crying because he's at his wits' end. His crying before, when he jumped down from the wall and fell, was nothing in comparison. We huddle together, most likely he feels just as cold as I do. He's probably a few months older.

I ask: "Shall we go into an empty house and lie down?"

He answers: "Are you crazy?" A few times my eyelids close. I think what a pity it is that it wasn't Julian who had the idea about the empty house. By now it's so light that my flashlight makes hardly more than a bright circle on the ground. I think of Father, wanting him to come and fetch us, first me, then Julian, or both together, one under each arm. I want him to lay me down on the bed and cover me up warmly: oh my, that would be good. He'd have to hold my Mother's hand. Both would have to stand beside the bed, looking down on me and smiling until I woke up.

Then something hurt. Before us stands a huge German. He has prodded me with his foot. He does it again, but not like someone meaning to kick. Out of his terrible eyes he utters a few words that are unintelligible; I'm too scared to try even to get up. Disaster won't really strike until I'm standing; I stay sitting down. But beside me Julian is on his feet, held up by his collar. The giant says in funny Polish: "What are you doing here?" I look at my friend; the giant shakes me a little.

Julian points at the wall and says: "We're from the camp." That makes me admire him for a long time—the calm way he says it. The giant asks: "And how did you get out?" Julian tells him the truth; meanwhile I look at the helmet and the rifle sticking up over the giant shoulder, the giant shoe on my stomach, pinning me down. I'm convinced we're soon going to be shot—we realized that from the beginning. The giant asks why the hell we didn't go back into our camp. Julian explains that too. He has never been as great a hero as now. The giant looks up to the top of the wall and seems to understand. He takes his foot away from my stomach—that's like an order to get up—and hardly am I on my feet when he grabs me by the collar. The flashlight is still lying on the ground. I have to get hold of it somehow before we leave.

The giant lets go of both of us and says: "Come with me to the guardhouse." But he just stands there without moving. So do we, of course—it's up to him to take the lead. "Come along, get a move on now," he says, giving us a shove. I turn toward the wall and pick up my flashlight—it's my last chance. The giant asks: "What've you got there?" and grabs my hands, which are behind my back. He sees the flashlight, takes it, tries it out, and puts it away in his pocket as if everything here belonged to him. Every bad thing I have ever heard about the Germans is suddenly true. I hate him like poison. If it had been anyone else I would have tried to persuade him to give me back the flashlight, even if it had meant an argument, even with Father. With this huge German it was hopeless. I see Julian stuff his shirt well down into his trousers. Only the two of us know what he is hiding under his shirt. I hope for his sake that he can hang onto his binoculars—I don't want the giant to have them. The giant says: "Get a move on now." He gives us another shove. We walk along in front of him. I notice Julian moving his booty from his back to his stomach. If we're going to be shot, I think, his binoculars won't be much use to him anyway. The giant tells us to stop.

With his giant hands he turns us around to face him. He looks at us for a long time, like a person with something on his mind—I wish him the worst worries in the world.

He says: "Do you know what'll happen to me if I don't take you to the guardhouse?" As if that concerned us: he's not only a thief, he's also an idiot. I think: Whatever happens to you, it can't be nearly bad enough.

Julian says: "No, I don't." I feel like answering that I don't care—it would be a good answer—but I see his great fists dangling. Oh how I'd love to be a giant! Suddenly, he grabs us both by the neck and flings himself on the ground, bringing us down with him. He is still holding me by the neck as if it were made of wood. He says: "Not a word." I see a light at the far end of the wall, a motorbike. Soon I can hear the sound of it; I seem to hear the giant's heart beating too; by now the pounding of his heart is louder than the sound of the motorbike. He says: "Not a word," though he's the only one talking. He's a thief, a fool, a coward—I'm not scared of someone like that. I can't see Julian because the huge body is lying between us. A long way off the motorbike turns a corner, but we have to stay where we are for a little while.

"Get up," the giant then says. He lets go of us and brushes off his soldier's clothes. I look at my underpants and know I'll be in plenty of trouble with my mother, if I ever get out of this alive. The giant takes off his helmet and wipes his forehead; like all Germans he has fair hair. He takes his time, as if the cold existed only for me and not for him. His helmet is back on his

42

head; now he takes hold of his rifle. This must be it: take you away and shoot you. They can do that.

Julian asks: "Are you going to shoot us now?"

The giant says nothing, probably doesn't consider Julian's question worth answering. He looks up and down the street; no doubt he doesn't want anyone to see what he is about to do to us. He says to Julian: "Don't you dare try and run away," and wags his finger at him. Why has he taken hold of his rifle if not to shoot us? But he leans it against the wall. I suppose he doesn't know himself what he wants. The flashlight is a little bulge under his jacket. I should have simply left it lying beside the wall, then one day some lucky person would have found it. He points at me and says only: "You there," and I have to go up to him. He says: "I'll lift you kids up onto the wall. But jump down quickly and run as fast as you can to your huts. Don't waste a second. Understand?" So that's what it's all about. I don't know whether I feel relieved—in a moment I'll have to jump again.

"We have a place," says Julian, "where there's no glass on top. It's not far from here."

The giant says: "There's no glass all along here," and lifts me up with no effort at all. I have no time to think about it; it hurts me because he's holding me by my hips. He says: "Stand on my shoulders." I lean against the wall and do as he tells me; I still can't reach the top. He says: "Now stand on my head." He holds me by my ankles; I pay him back a bit for the flashlight: I make myself heavy and don't try to spare his head. The helmet is his salvation, without a helmet he'd have a surprise coming to him. He says: "Hurry up." I stand on one leg—there's not room on the helmet—now I can grab the top of the wall. He asks: "Can you hold on?" I cautiously lift my foot from his head and he moves away from under me. I hang there, and will never get onto the wall; it's exactly how I hung there before, except that then I wanted to get down to the ground and not get to the top. I look down over my shoulder and see him pick up his rifle.

That's the ultimate shock. No one can imagine: to be hanging up there in the air just for him to shoot me, after all those nice speeches. There's nothing to hold me to the wall now; I let go. As the years pass, the fall gets longer and longer—no wall can be that high—then I am caught by the giant. It is as if I had never fallen. The giant puts his hand over my mouth before I can scream. He says: "What d'you think you're doing?" He sets me on my feet, picks up his rifle from the ground, and props it against the wall again. Then he says: "Once more, quick now." Again he lifts me up, already I feel a bit more at home on his shoulders. This time I leave his head in peace. The sight of Julian standing down below makes me feel envious: I'm fighting a life-and-death struggle. I fall and I'll be shot or not shot, and he stands there looking on, calm as you please. And he's even allowed to keep his binoculars. I'll have to have a word with him about that later.

Once again I grab the top of the wall. The giant lets go of one ankle, the other remains in his hand. He says to Julian: "Give me the rifle." He presses the rifle butt against my behind and pushes me up. I can almost sit on it. With no effort I manage to get onto the wall. I lie on my stomach and can see how right he was—there's not even the tiniest scrap of glass in sight; the glass is a mystery. I can look into our camp where it is still as silent and empty as at night, though it's as light as day now. The giant calls from below: "Get down there!"

I turn around on the wall, hang down on the other side, and fall until I can fall no further. I lie there crying. I am back again and have brought nothing with me but sore places. Julian is no longer of interest to me; in the future he'll have to find others for his ideas. I stand up. My parents feel closer. Father will be glad I'm still alive, my Mother will cry when she sees me, then she'll wash out my many wounds; I won't be able to tell them the truth. My hands are bleeding again, my knees are bleeding, my elbow looks as if it has been dipped in dirt and blood. One consolation is that they'll probably feel so sorry for me they'll stroke me. I start walking. Tomorrow I'll say to Julian: "So all Germans sleep at night, do they?"

As I turn around, he jumps down from the wall by his own method. Though it's not a bad fall, he doesn't get up. Seeing him lying there on his stomach, I go back to him because he's my friend. He's crying, crying, and crying—I have never seen anyone cry like that before. I had already finished crying, now I start up again myself. I ask: "Did he take away the binoculars?" It is a while before he pushes my hand away and gets up. I can see the binoculars under his shirt. He limps away, crying all the time. I run after him and at last feel superior. I ask: "Are we going to meet tomorrow?" I see nothing wrong with this question, but what does Julian do? He hits me over the head. He looks at me as if he had more blows for me in his fists, then he limps on again. I stay where I am and can still hear him crying; I needn't be that sorry for him that I have to run after him again. I'm looking forward to the hut, where I won't have to feel cold any more.

Beyond the door it is dark. I close it so softly that I hear nothing; anyone who wasn't awake before will still be asleep. My parents are sitting on the bed, staring at me wide-eyed.

Someone whispers: "Good God, what have they done to you?"

Right now nothing hurts any more, yet I feel as if the worst is still to come. My Mother holds both hands over her mouth. Father doesn't move. I stand between his knees. He puts one hand on my head and turns me around. Then he holds me by both shoulders and asks: "Where have you been?"

I say: "I was outside and fell down."

Father says: "No one falls down like that." My Mother has risen and is searching in our brown carry-all. Father shakes me so violently that my head, which for a long time had given me no trouble, begins hurting again.

I say: "We met outside and had a fight and beat each other up. That's the truth."

He asks: "Who's 'we'?"

I say: "You don't know him." Suddenly I can lie as never before. My Mother is holding a dripping towel. She takes me away from Father and leads me to the light by the window. Father follows us and looks on.

"Go and ask Professor Engländer whether he can come and look at him," says my Mother.

Father asks: "Can't we wait till after inspection?"

"No," she retorts, "or daren't you go outside?" Off he goes on tiptoe, and at last my Mother strokes me. She says: "You must realize that he's upset."

She lays me down on the bed and nurses my head on her lap. I think that later perhaps I'll tell her the truth, only her. She says: "How tired you are, my little one." It is bliss to lie in her lap, though her finger won't let me fall asleep. She speaks to someone, a few times I hear the word "probably." I open my eyes and she is smiling down at me as if I were something funny.

Father is holding a little dark bottle in his hand. "Engländer gave me some iodine," he says.

I ask: "Will it hurt?"

My Mother says: "Yes, but it can't be helped." So I get up and back away because in my opinion enough things have hurt this past night.

Father says: "Don't listen to her, it won't hurt. It just cleans out the wound." That sounds a bit better. He says: "I can prove it." I watch very carefully—after all it's my pain—I look at his outstretched arm. He dribbles a few drops from the bottle onto his arm; they form a little black lake and slowly spread. Then he says: "That's supposed to hurt? Do you think I would put the stuff on my own arm if it hurt?" I look into his eyes from very close up and can't see even the tiniest trace of pain. A further proof is that my Mother goes away; she was wrong and doesn't want to admit it, so she simply goes away. Father says: "Come here now." I hold out my elbow to him, he twists my arm a little so that the drops fall straight into the wound.

Translated by Leila Vennewitz

The Tale of the
Sick Princess

from *Jacob the Liar*

Lina is in luck. Jacob soon finds the station where fairy tales are being told by a kindly uncle who says: "For all the children listening to us, your fairy-tale uncle will tell you the story of the sick princess."

"Do you know that one?" Jacob asks as Jacob.

"No. But how can there be a fairy-tale uncle on the radio?"

"What do you mean, how? There is, that's all."

"But you said radio was forbidden for children. And fairy tales are only for children, aren't they?"

"True. But what I meant was that it's forbidden here in the ghetto. Where there's no ghetto, children are allowed to listen. And there are radios everywhere. Right?"

"Right."

The fairy-tale uncle, a bit put out by the interruption but fair enough to look for the reasons in himself, takes off his jacket and puts it under him, since the bucket is hard and sharp edged and the fairy tale one of the longer ones—provided, that is, he can remember how it all goes.

"When's it going to start?" Lina asks.

"The tale of the sick princess," the fairy-tale uncle begins.

About the good old king who had a vast country and a gloriously beautiful palace and a daughter as well, the old story, and how he got a terrible scare. Because, you see, he loved her more than anything in the world, his princess. He loved her so much that, whenever she fell and tears came into her eyes, he had to cry himself. And the scare came when one morning she didn't want to get out of bed and looked really sick. Then the most expensive doctor in all the land was summoned to make her well quickly and happy again. But the doctor tapped and listened to her from head to toe and then said in great perplexity: "I'm terribly sorry, Mr. King, I can't find anything. Your daughter must be suffering from a disease I have never come across during my entire lifetime."

Now the good old king was even more scared, so he went to see the princess himself and asked her what on earth was the matter. And she told him she wanted a cloud: once she had that, she would be well again immediately. "But a real one!" she said. What a shock that was, for, as anyone can imagine, it is far from easy to get hold of a real cloud, even for a king. All day long he was so worried that he couldn't rule, and that evening he had letters sent out to all the clever men in his kingdom ordering them to drop everything and come forthwith to the royal palace.

Next morning they were all assembled, the doctors and the ministers, the stargazers and the weathermen, and the king stood up on his throne so that everyone in the hall could hear him properly and shouted: "Si—lence!" Instantly you could have heard a pin drop, and the king announced: "To the one among you wise men who brings my daughter a cloud from the sky I will give as much gold and silver as can be heaped onto the biggest wagon in all the land!" When the clever men heard that, they started then and there to study, to ponder, to scheme, and to calculate. For they all wanted that heap of gold and silver, who wouldn't? One especially smart fellow even began building a tower that was to reach up to the clouds, the idea being that, when the tower was finished, he would climb up, grab a cloud, and then cash in the reward. But before the tower was even halfway up, it fell down. And none of the others had any luck either; not one of the wise men could get the princess the cloud she so badly wanted. She grew thinner and sicker, thinner and thinner, since from sheer misery she never touched a morsel, not even matzo with butter.

One fine day the garden boy, who the princess sometimes used to play with outdoors before she got sick, looked into the palace to see whether any of the vases needed flowers. So it came about that he saw her lying in her bed, under a silken coverlet, pale as snow. All through the last few days he had been puzzling over why she never came out into the garden anymore. And that is why he asked her, "What is the matter, little princess? Why don't you come out into the sunshine anymore?" And so she told him, too, that she was sick and wouldn't get well again until someone brought her a cloud. The garden boy thought for a bit, then exclaimed, "But that's quite easy, little princess!" "Is it?" the princess asked in surprise. "Is it quite easy? All the wise men in the land have been racking their brains in vain, and you claim that it's quite easy?" "Yes," the garden boy said, "you just have to tell me what a cloud is made of." That would have almost made the princess laugh if she hadn't been so weak. She replied, "What silly questions you ask! Everybody knows that clouds are made of cotton!" "I see, and will you also tell me how big a cloud is?" "You don't even know *that*?" she said in surprise. "A cloud is as big as my pillow. You can see that for yourself if you'll just pull the curtain aside and look up at the sky." Whereupon the garden boy went to the window, looked up at the sky, and exclaimed, "You're right! Just as big as your pillow!" Then he went off and soon returned, bringing the princess a piece of cotton as big as her pillow.

I needn't bother with the rest. Everyone can easily imagine how the princess's eyes lit up and her lips turned red and she got well again, how the good old king rejoiced, how the garden boy didn't want the promised reward but preferred to marry the princess, and they lived happily ever after. That's Jacob's story.

* * *

Jacob stands motionless at the little opening, his whole attention absorbed by the passing countryside. Lina taps his leg.

He looks down and asks, "What is it?"

"Do you remember the fairy tale?" she asks.

"Which one?"

"About the sick princess?"

"Yes."

"Is it true?"

It is clear from his expression that he finds it strange for her to be thinking of that just now.

"Of course it's true," he says.

"But Siegfried and Rafi wouldn't believe me."

"Maybe you didn't tell it properly?"

"I told it exactly as you did. But they say there's no such thing in the whole world."

"No such thing as what?"

"That a person can get well again by being given a bunch of cotton."

Jacob bends down and lifts her up to the little window.

"But it's true, isn't it?" says Lina. "The princess wanted a bunch of cotton as big as a pillow? And when she had it she got well again?"

I see Jacob's mouth widen, and he says, "Not exactly. She wished for a cloud. The point is that she thought clouds are made of cotton, and that's why she was satisfied with cotton."

Lina looks out for a while, surprised, it seems to me, before asking him: "But aren't clouds made of cotton?"

Translated by Leila Vennewitz

The Most Popular Family Story

I can't say it doesn't bother me that the tradition I'm about to relate both came into existence and vanished before my time. In those days our family was still extensive—the term "vast" suggests itself—and an occasion of some importance was needed to gather all its members in one place. Ordinary birthdays were not enough. My only bridge to this time, which I feel is most accurately described as "in those days," was my father. When he passed away, I felt that I hadn't been sufficiently informed about what it was like "in those days." The information I did receive seemed more precious than ever all of a sudden. I knew nothing more would be added—by whom?—and I began to regard the few stories as a treasure to be handled with care.

It was usually births that brought the entire family together, not that anyone decided it should be that way. But, as my father recalled, more often than not the cries of a newborn would accompany these events. Coincidence? he once asked me, who had attended only my own birth. He waited for a moment and began shaking his head, as if convinced that whatever my theories about the answer to his question, they were of exceptional stupidity. However, if it was not a coincidence, he asked, then what was the reason? I sat there, acting as if it pained me not to know the answer, and after I had shrugged my shoulders enough he revealed why it is that births present the ideal occasion for family gatherings. First, they happen only infrequently, much more so than birthdays, for example. Second, every decent human being feels the desire to see and touch and kiss a new family member. A sense of family, according to my father, was more than a mere theory. Third, they allow those in attendance—after admiring the newborn child and handing over their gifts—to swiftly and without delay sit down to fulfill the actual purpose of the gathering. They can ask about each other's health, how business is going, and what news has emerged since the last birth. No one feels overlooked by this: not the baby—obviously—not the mother, who is busy with her child and her gifts, and also not the father, who is either drunk or in a serendipitous stupor. And lastly, my father explained to me, births have a tendency to induce a certain gleefulness in those present as soon as the door is opened before them. It is likely because of this that some stories were never told at these gatherings, while others were retold time and time again.

Uncle Gideon, the owner of the most popular family story, must have been an impressive man. At large events, isn't it true that there are usually a hundred different conversations going on at the same time, and what might sound like an incomprehensible hubbub to someone who has just entered the room in fact conveys a hundred different meanings? Yet when Uncle Gideon spoke, the others went silent. He wasn't the richest member of the family, not at all. Nor was he the poorest. Nevertheless, no one had to fear hardship were they to fall out of favor with him. Before he would tell the story, there always had to be a substantial amount of pleading; everyone knew this. They pleaded with him as though the pleading were part of the story, as though he couldn't start before he had been pleaded with enough. Then everyone felt the moment approach when it was Uncle Gideon's turn to say: Very well.

He was quite an old man already when his story achieved such renown. My father would describe to me his mouth and the scar on his forehead and his hair, and also the way he dressed and what his hands were doing while he was telling the story. Once my father said, Gideon was a very old man when they took him to Majdanek, but still.

I don't know why the story became so popular. Sometimes I feel like I heard it before, a long time ago, without my Uncle Gideon in it; but I may be mistaken. I think it's not a bad story, but not a great one either. Its remarkable success must have stemmed from Uncle Gideon's charisma, or from the taste of those who lived in those days. In any case, the reason remains obscure to me. My father told it to me ten or twenty times, as if he felt obliged to continue a tradition that the story must be retold again and again. Only a force as powerful as death itself could stop it. And because on the one hand I don't want to be an ungrateful son to my father, and on the other I have no intention of holding onto this same story for as long as that, I'm setting it down now to get it off my chest. Every time he told it, my father would act as though he were telling it for the first time. He wanted to feel my curiosity, to savor my surprise and keep me in suspense again and again. I have to admit, whether I want to or not, that every time I heard Uncle Gideon's story I enjoyed it a little more.

Before I continue, there is one last obstacle to overcome, or rather, I would like to say how I intend to circumvent it. That is to say, the story has many versions. Whenever my father told it to me, it was different, albeit always revolving around Uncle Gideon, of course, who—in every version—had to travel to London on business. Nearly everything beyond that needs to be treated with caution. Most of the essential details in telling the story may be more accurately described as median values. I have calculated them myself, taking into account the deviations that occurred in every direction when my father told the story. Sadly, I'm only just now—much too late—beginning to ask myself whether Uncle Gideon himself may not have been at the origin of the different versions; and whether in the end it may be this very circumstance that lay at the heart of the story's puzzling success. This, then, is the most popular family story:

In the winter of 1922, Uncle Gideon travels to London. His journey is not for pleasure, as a stranger might presume. Two machines need to be procured for the hosiery factory of which Gideon—for all intents and purposes—is the director. Uncle Gideon hates traveling.

He has never before really left Lublin, despite having almost reached the age of sixty. One time he made it to Lviv, a few times as far as Krakow, not counting the occasional holiday—usually spent in Sopot. Uncle Gideon likes to say: Traveling is the pastime of the dissatisfied. He likes to add: He who cannot find the world at home is also not at home in the world. These words are followed by a short silence, after which Uncle Gideon takes a cigar and places it between his teeth. The order remains unchanged, and in the short pause between the two sentences, Uncle Menachem has already reached for the box of matches. Anyway, Uncle Gideon feels more comfortable at home than anywhere else. As if to prove it, he looks at his wife, Aunt Linda, and at that moment everyone looks at her, too. And already a faint smile is making the rounds, because Aunt Linda is just a little too intimidating for Uncle Gideon's words to be completely believable. Ultimately, he may mean the exact opposite, though no one knows for sure, and even Aunt Linda is smiling and appears to be flattered by her husband's praise.

So Uncle Gideon reluctantly travels to London and during the crossing is already plagued by a strange feeling. The water is calm, and fear of seasickness unwarranted. Uncle Gideon carries with him three different types of medication, for he has suffered from a weak stomach from a young age. The steward spills coffee on the plaid blanket that's spread over Uncle Gideon's lap but removes it quickly enough that his trousers—the dark brown ones made of Belgian wool, Aunt Linda interjects—remain untouched. London is shrouded in fog, like one reads about in the magazines. Uncle Gideon is not surprised. He takes a hackney carriage to his hotel. He can barely see what is right in front of him, yet the English cabbie hurtles on at speeds that would be appropriate only in the best of weather. It costs him his tip.

The hotel room is like a hotel room; the food, however, is nothing like dinner. It begins with his fruitless search for a kosher restaurant, which he abandons after an hour. Uncle Gideon won't go as far as to say that there is not a single kosher restaurant in all of London, but what he is willing to say is that such a restaurant, should it exist, is nearly impossible for a stranger to find. He goes to bed hungry, until his weak stomach, as we recall, puts an end to his piousness. Uncle Gideon wanders about his dreary room, not prepared for the stomachache but expecting it any moment. Suddenly, he is halted by the question of how he is supposed to survive a week in London without food. He doesn't find an answer and thus puts the question to God. Even He needs to think it over. Following a lengthy debate, carried on in a friendly fashion, Uncle Gideon removes his hairnet and makes his way downstairs to the restaurant. The God of the Jews is an understanding one, Uncle Gideon says; He can be reasoned with. But not another word about English food at the hotel, Uncle Gideon continues, brushing aside the thought with one hand while the other pats his belly. He says: If only the food were as easy to swallow as it was to forget.

Back to the matter at hand: Uncle Gideon's plan is to stay in London for one week. After three days, however, the machines are already purchased—at a bargain price, of course: send Uncle Gideon to buy something and he'll come back to you with more money than you gave him. Uncle Julian, red in the face with excitement, shouts, Gideon, you fiend, why the devil won't you become my partner? Uncle Gideon calmly responds: Let's discuss it another time, when you have your books with you. It'll be easier to explain then. Of course, everyone is laughing again, Uncle Julian the loudest. After all, what was he expecting, asking such a question?

Uncle Gideon, meanwhile, has another four days in London and doesn't know what to do with them. Already he has visited most of the sights—nobody can negotiate day and night—the Queen's palace, certain towers, certain bridges, also a square with an Italian name that is almost as busy as the market in Lublin but doesn't smell nearly as good. Museums are not Uncle Gideon's thing. He begins to wonder whether it might not be best to let London be London and whether the last four days might be better spent returning to Lublin early, whether he shouldn't just get on the next train and cross his legs. On the other hand, the hotel room has been paid for in advance and on the third day the room also doesn't feel as foreign anymore. Furthermore, changing his ticket reservation would require assistance; no one here seems to understand Gideon's English. And finally, all things considered, how often do you visit London? Fog or no, it is London. Uncle Gideon decides that fear and homesickness are inappropriate for a man his age. He remains in London—thank God, as my father says—giving the following events a chance to unfold.

At least the English know their tea. Tea they take seriously. Uncle Gideon lives on tea and cake, which seems to be slightly less unbearable than the other fare. Even though he never eats sweets at home, Aunt Linda would sometimes add ruefully. On the fourth day our uncle discovers that he needs to cinch his belt a whole lot tighter. Should this make him happy or not? Aunt Linda says: When he came back, I had to move the buttons on all his pants by this much. Uncle Gideon nods then says: But four weeks later they had to go back to where they were before.

On the fifth day, Uncle Gideon feels a heavy hand on his shoulder just as he is stepping out of the hotel to take a walk. A man named Silverstone, one of the people with whom he had negotiated, is holding him back. Silverstone says: Hello, old boy (this is how they all speak in England), I thought you were already back on your lousy continent?

For a moment, Uncle Gideon understands the use of the word "lousy" to be an expression of prejudice about the hygienic conditions in Galicia. He raises an eyebrow and is about to respond that only last night he had to kill no less than four bedbugs in his fancy hotel room, when he realizes that Silverstone is merely expressing himself in the casual manner that is so commonplace and meant nothing by it. One time Aunt Annette asks: Say, Gideon, did you really find four bedbugs in your hotel room? And Uncle Gideon says to her: Is that of any importance?

Silverstone learns of Uncle Gideon's intention to stay in London for a few days and that he doesn't have any plans, at which he exclaims: Why didn't you say something?

Uncle Gideon describes him as a man who talks a lot but doesn't say very much, a circumstance that greatly helped in the negotiations. Our uncle is immediately forced to be his guest and joins him at a teahouse, even though he just finished his breakfast tea. But for Silverstone, tea is merely an excuse to drink whisky. He orders a large glass for each of them, before noon, on a normal weekday—such is the state of affairs in England. Even today, Uncle Gideon shudders when he remembers having to force the whisky down his throat, sip after sip, his protests in vain. To cope with the memory, he empties a small glass of vodka, in little sips, and my father winks at me: how Gideon knows to tell his story.

So Mr. Silverstone likes to drink, no matter the time of day. Uncle Gideon has to drink with him, and his stomach is holding up surprisingly well, but never again will he travel abroad. Silverstone showers him with advice on what he should see on his last two days in London, but Uncle Gideon knows immediately that he isn't interested in any of it. Dog racing, he says, and lifts his shoulders up to his ears. Can you imagine, he asks, a grown man bringing himself to ruin, because one dog can run faster than another? He has made plans for his last night anyway: Mendelssohn at Royal Albert Hall. At least his English will not put him at a disadvantage there.

In the afternoon—London is already spinning rather fast around his head—he feels like taking a nap, but Silverstone won't allow it. Without mercy he leads Uncle Gideon from one establishment to another, persists in buying fresh rounds, and fancies himself the greatest of hosts. For a moment our uncle considers whether this may be Silverstone's way of getting his revenge, because the negotiations had not gone as he had anticipated. But he immediately dismisses the thought: there is no way Silverstone is that cunning. One has only to look at him. He is clearly motivated by cordiality, even if it is a cordiality that is difficult to bear.

Suddenly, on the street and between drinks, Silverstone slaps Uncle Gideon on the back so hard he almost falls over. I've got it! he shouts, and Uncle Gideon—startled—asks: *What* have you got? Silverstone, however, just stands there, smiling and shaking his head like someone who is almost choking on a good idea but not yet ready to share it. That alone should have aroused Uncle Gideon's suspicions. Today he knows, today he is the wiser. In those days, he simply attributes everything this Silverstone does to that peculiar English way of behaving.

Silverstone asks: What do you think, old friend, about going to my club? By now Uncle Gideon has given up. He knows with certainty there would be no use in saying, I think perhaps not. He replies: To the club then. Silverstone starts walking in a different direction, along a number of crooked streets, along a number of straight ones, and suddenly he stops. Suddenly, he wants to know whether Uncle Gideon has ever been to a costume party. A costume party? our astounded uncle says, the things you say.

It turns out that Silverstone has just remembered that he is invited to a costume party tomorrow, the best costume party in all of London. But, unfortunately, tomorrow of all days he has an important meeting with a Turkish business partner. His company does business all over the world. If, however, Uncle Gideon were to take his place, he can offer every assurance that the hosts would be most pleased, and honored besides. Uncle Gideon repeats: The things you say.

Then they are sitting at the club, about which there is not much to say except that, in Lublin, it wouldn't survive one month. In one of the rooms, Uncle Gideon notices chess players. He watches them play for a moment and soon realizes how easily he could defeat most of them. Nevertheless, he refrains from joining them, for they are playing in a ridiculously serious manner, sitting in grim silence and darting evil glances at anyone who dares speak an innocent word. Silverstone keeps coming back to the costume party, and our uncle keeps shaking his head. At the same time, he has begun to ask himself why he is so vehemently opposed to the idea. He also wonders: What else am I going to do? I'm not interested in the churches, nor in the palaces, nor in the exhibitions. Why did I stay here, if not to learn about the customs and traditions of these peculiar people? Uncle Gideon asks himself all this and finally he asks Silverstone: But in what language should I speak with these people?

In that moment, Silverstone knows he has won. Beaming and brimming with guilelessness, he answers that the hosts speak, if not Polish, at least excellent German. Much too late, only today in fact, Uncle Gideon asks himself what there is to beam about when someone else is taking your place at a costume party. I can hear Mendelssohn at home, he thinks back then, and probably better than in London. Silverstone is already writing down the hosts' name and address. He'll call them first thing tomorrow morning, so they know to expect Uncle Gideon.

During the course of the evening, our uncle asks what the local custom is with respect to costumes. He shouldn't worry about it too much, he's told, one simply wears whatever one can get one's hands on. He, Silverstone, tends to go with a mere suggestion of a costume. A little hat would suffice, or a cardboard nose, says Silverstone and falls into a fit of laughter. Should, however, Uncle Gideon—with respect to the costume—feel any sort of ambition, there is bound to be a costume rental near the hotel. Costume rentals in London are a dime a dozen. Uncle Gideon as Genghis Khan, Silverstone says, and has another laughing fit, and even our uncle is amused by the notion *in those days.* And as they are sitting and drinking and later on eating and conversing, there comes a moment when Uncle Gideon begins to feel distinctly and with conviction that to be invited to a costume party may actually be the best thing that could possibly happen to a stranger in London.

The next day arrives and already the morning begins with a bundle of worry for our uncle. He is lying comfortably on his back when he is suddenly confronted by the thought: What business does a Jew from Lublin have attending an English costume party? He struggles with the question for a few minutes, until he thinks of a different one: Why should a Jew from Lublin not attend an English costume party? This question appears more convincing to him. It isn't as wary of the unfamiliar. And in the bathtub he begins to think about what he should wear. At breakfast he remembers the old principle that has made him who he is today: If you are going to do something, do it right. As a result, the waiter has to go and find the address of the nearest costume rental. As Silverstone predicted, it is not far.

Our uncle wanders between clothes racks and is unsure how best to decide. He is in no mood to become a pirate or a bandit, or a king or nobleman. He nearly decides to go to the party as Uncle Gideon from Lublin or not at all, when he is gripped by an old dream from his childhood, right there in front of the shelf with the head wear: to be the sad pale clown that everyone at the circus laughs at because he doesn't understand a thing but thinks himself the smartest of all. He rents everything he needs, the pantaloons, a silver silk shirt with large black buttons, the pointy hat with the chinstrap. Back at the hotel, he realizes that a clown not only wears certain clothes but also has a certain face, a very white face with round black eyes. So Uncle Gideon goes out and buys some white makeup and some black makeup, and Aunt Linda shakes her head at the crazy ideas her Gideon used to have.

He spends half the day in front of the mirror, getting dressed and painting his face. It takes a long time before his face looks the way he remembers it should. The eyes, he says, the eyes drove me to despair. Again and again, he washes the makeup off his face until finally—with his skin starting to redden—he takes a piece of paper and practices. Only after a while does he realize his mistake: he was painting the eyelashes as though they were normal eyelashes, when he really should have painted them as short, thick lines, like the rays of a child's sun. And under each eye there must be a small, round spot—God knows why—which gives the face a bewildered, and somehow sad, expression. Uncle Gideon transfers his design from the paper to his face, and in the end he is satisfied. He would be lying if he said, Uncle Gideon confesses, that he was not reluctant at first to step out of the hotel room in his outfit. But how else, he asks, was he to get to the costume party, and no one has an answer. Of course, he drapes his long coat over everything. He puts on his regular hat, which everyone knows. The pointy hat is wrapped in paper and tucked under his arm. He walks down the stairs, does not see a single person, and the lobby is also empty. Uncle Gideon's resolve not to feel embarrassed by any mocking looks was needless, for until he reaches the street he is met by no such looks. It is already dark, and fortunately it's not raining, so he needn't worry about his face. He enters a cab, and he says: In London you have to watch what you do with your hands. Why? As soon as you hold one out, a taxi will stop. He shows the address to the driver; the driver nods and knows the way.

Then Uncle Gideon is standing before a mansion on the edge of town. Laughter begins to spread around the room, because everyone is anticipating what is about to follow; and whoever doesn't anticipate, at least knows. By now the ladies are beginning to search in their purses for a handkerchief, as our uncle picks his way across the English garden toward the house. He stops one last time to count the windows—only the lit ones—and arrives at a number no one would believe. And before he knocks, he encounters one last problem: the hats. He stands there, with one on his head and the other tucked under his arm, but Uncle Gideon doesn't want to end up being someone who stands before the door with a hat in each hand. He needs to keep one of them on his head; he is merely unsure which one. After a moment to consider, he makes a decision. He puts the clown hat on his head, wraps the regular hat in the paper, and hides it in a bush next to the entrance. Uncle Gideon thinks he can hear music inside, but he may be mistaken. He rings the doorbell, and when he hears steps inside, our Uncle Marian stands up from his chair to listen to the remainder of the story on his feet.

The door is opened by a butler, like the ones at the municipal theater in Lublin. For a second Uncle Gideon thinks the person in front of him is a guest at the costume party, just like himself. The man asks him a question, which of course Uncle Gideon fails to understand, but the meaning of which he determines with great presence of mind. He retrieves a business card from his pocket and places it on the little tray the butler is presenting to him, which—if our uncle isn't mistaken—is made of silver. Finally, he is let through, but Uncle Gideon misjudges the height of the door-frame. His hat catches, slides back, and the chinstrap chokes him a little. The butler closes the door. He says some more words, offers our uncle a seat, and walks off with the business card. But Uncle Gideon doesn't sit down. Instead, he concentrates on the mirror hung on the wall. He rearranges his hat, inspects his shirt. Most importantly, however, he examines his face, with which he is still content, except for a spot on his fore-head where the makeup has inexplicably vanished. From afar, he hears the voice of an English child and in that same moment realizes that there is no music playing in the house, contrary to his initial impression. For the first time, he senses a touch of unease, but he doesn't yet know why. But Uncle Menachem, clasping his tie, already shouts: Go into the room already, we can't take it any longer!

The butler returns, still failing to realize our uncle doesn't understand his language. He takes Uncle Gideon's coat. At least Uncle Gideon understands this. It means: They are expecting you. He follows the butler around many corners to a large, not very well lit room that is rather chilly, like all rooms in England, apparently. Turning away from the fireplace, the host, an unremarkable man, like dozens he saw at the club, approaches Uncle Gideon. He holds out his hand, which Uncle Gideon takes. The host conveys—in reasonably good German—how extraordinarily pleased he is by our uncle's visit. Uncle Gideon thanks him for the invitation in the same language, although he is slightly puzzled by his host's rather unimaginative costume: a black dinner jacket, gray pants, a white shirt, a tie, and nothing else. Only then does he notice the lady of the house sitting in an armchair, and he goes to her. With a charming smile, she holds out her hand in such a way that Uncle Gideon is expected to kiss it, this much he understands. He does so, at the same time using his free hand to hold on to his hat, which is not secured tightly enough for a bow. The lady's dress seems more original; it is a floor-length red gown with a lace collar, just as the fine ladies in Galicia wore them seventy or eighty years ago. No one else is there yet.

Uncle Gideon sits in an armchair by the fireplace, annoyed that he arrived so early, probably because Silverstone told him the wrong hour. The butler continues to torture him by asking more questions; he looks for help. His host translates, inquiring whether he desires sherry or port wine or tea, and Uncle Gideon decides for tea, as long as he is the only guest. Then, while they are waiting for the drinks, Uncle Gideon discovers a dog lying in the room. I say "dog," Uncle Gideon corrects himself, holding up his wine glass for someone to fill. In Lublin we would call it a horse. Then he looks around and sees that there are no glasses set up around the room, and no bottles, and also that there are no chairs for other guests. What kind of costume party is this going to be? And for the second time, Uncle Gideon feels unease, this time rather intensely.

My father, if I may weave this in, was always pretty much in stitches by this point, usually even before. Most of the time I didn't appear sufficiently amused to him, but this was never a great hindrance. Only once did he sigh and stop talking, until at last I asked him what was wrong. He then confided to me that he would much rather have the story told to him than tell it. For a long moment, I considered whether I should offer to switch roles. But I abandoned the idea, because somehow it seemed improper. He might not even have accepted. By this time, he had already resumed the story and was demonstrating how our uncle was sitting there, with his pointy hat and his tea. The host inquires whether this is Uncle Gideon's first time in London. He then asks how long our uncle has known Silverstone. Uncle Gideon tells him the truth: For some time in correspondence, but only for a few days in person. The host exchanges a glance with his lady, a disconcertingly long one, then he smiles somberly and says: He was always a rather strange man, this Mr. Silverstone.

From one moment to the next, our uncle decides to get rid of the hat at all costs. He thinks: Surely, I can do without that. He leans forward and puts his cup of tea down on a small table, when the dog raises its head and growls at him. The horse! shouts Aunt Esther or Aunt Moira, and brutally slaps whoever is sitting in front of her on the shoulder. Uncle Gideon, however, follows through with his plan: he undoes the chinstrap, removes the hat, and sets it down on the floor next to his chair. At that same moment he feels a relief of the kind that we—having never been in such a situation— cannot possibly understand.

The lady inquires whether Uncle Gideon is enjoying London. He doesn't tell her the complete truth, but praises London as though he had to sell it. He merely laments a little the English way of eating, which should be allowed after his torment. The lady counters that taste is a matter of habit. It is quite understandable that everyone would think their local cuisine the best. Uncle Gideon disputes this. He entreats the lady to imagine a man who came down to earth—say from the moon—and compares English cuisine with, say, the French. The host says: The man from the moon would prefer the French way of cooking, I am sure of it. Uncle Gideon smiles politely; it is not in his manner to argue needlessly. Gradually, he begins to ponder what drove Silverstone to do this to him. The butler returns with fresh tea. Our uncle takes his cup from the table and adds, English tea, however, is the best by far.

He hears the doorbell ring. His heart skips a beat at the thought of new guests arriving. Now, it's time for the toreros and the Helens of Troy. Secretly, he is already rescinding his death threats against Silverstone. He looks at the hat on the floor, which, in a moment—if all goes well—will be back in service. The host and his lady exchange a few words. Uncle Gideon sips his tea and strains his ears. The door opens, unfortunately, behind Uncle Gideon, who musters just enough self-restraint not to turn his head. The lady, in her language, speaks a few words past Uncle Gideon, which, judging by the tone of her voice, are of a chastising nature. If our uncle isn't mistaken, her words are directed at a child. He brings himself to overcome his restraint and turns his head, but too late. The only thing he sees is the door handle snapping back into its position. The host apologizes for the small incident, and Uncle Gideon hasn't even understood what happened. From this moment onward, he finds it increasingly difficult to speak, as the thought of Silverstone grows more and more powerful.

You poor, poor man, says Aunt Miriam, and no one knows whether she is close to tears or laughter. Uncle Menachem says: I would have killed him, I swear to you, I would've killed him! Uncle Gideon replies: That was my only thought that night.

From now on, our uncle can concentrate only on survival. He is of no use for conversation anymore and barely participates. From time to time, he shoots Silverstone or pushes him off a very high mountain. He replies only with yes or no and is a terrible guest, until, unexpectedly, he is gripped by a strong pity for his hosts. He imagines how someone must feel who is expecting a normal guest, and then, through no fault of their own, receives *him*. He imagines how terrified they must have been as he stood there in the door, with his hat and his crazy eyes and all the rest. How they must have taken him for a lunatic, possibly, before asking themselves whether the poor Jews of Galicia always dress like that. How they must count this evening among the inexplicable events of their lives and yet act as though there was nothing unusual to it. No, our uncle thinks, this is more than mere politeness. This is admirable.

He should explain to them, he thinks soon after. But then he feels his pride and thinks: The one who's responsible should do the explaining. When a clock begins to strike the hour, Uncle Gideon stands up from his chair. He has plans for a concert, he says, Mendelssohn at Royal Albert Hall, and he has to stop by his hotel beforehand to change his clothes. His hosts are very understanding. The lady thanks him for his charming visit. Doing so, she doesn't seem like someone who says one thing and thinks another. The host firmly shakes our uncle's hand. The dog is nowhere to be seen. In saying his goodbyes, Uncle Gideon reminds them that his address is on his business card, and if they ever were to find themselves in Lublin, they shouldn't hesitate.

Then he stands before the house and doesn't remember exactly in which bush he had hidden his wonderful gray trilby. He takes a deep breath of the cold air and walks along the dark street toward a brighter one, while his audience begins to calm down after his adventure. Some are starting to feel hungry, the smell spreading from the kitchen is magnificent, and Uncle Gideon holds his hand out to hail a taxi. As he sits down in the car, he sneezes, leaving white marks on his handkerchief. In memory of his trip to London, he has kept the little boxes with the black and white makeup. Now, he recalls, he had promised to bring them this time. They must excuse him, he is an old man, and next time—with Aunt Linda's help—he will be sure to remember.

Translated by Jonathan Becker

The Suspect

I ask you to believe me when I say that I find the security of the state something worth protecting at almost all costs. I say this not to cajole anyone or in the hope that a certain agency might be more favorably disposed to me as a result. I simply feel the need to express it, even though, for some time now, I've been considered a person who presents a danger to that very security.

The fact that I've come to have such a reputation both shocks and embarrasses me. To my knowledge, I have never given the slightest cause for suspicion of any kind. I've been a committed citizen since childhood, or at least I've tried to be. I can't recall a single circumstance when I might have uttered an opinion that doesn't correspond to those held by the state, and therefore to my own; and if this ever did happen, it could only have been due to a lack of concentration on my part. I would hope the gaze of the state is trained and discerning enough to recognize real threats and disregard trifles that are anything but threatening. And yet something must have occurred near me that caused the state to direct some of its attention my way. Maybe some will understand me when I say that, at this point, I'm glad not to know what it was. If I did, most likely I'd try to counteract the unfavorable impression and make matters worse in the process. This way, however, I can move more freely, or at least I'm getting there.

By now it will have become clear that I'm under surveillance. My situation is complicated by the crucial fact that, in principle, I consider this sort of procedure useful, indispensable even. Yet, in my case it's pointless and, be honest, insulting.

One day, a man named Bogelin, whom I had regarded until then as loyal to the government, told me that I was under observation. Naturally, I immediately ceased all dealings with him. I didn't believe a word he said and thought: Under observation, me! I had almost forgotten about the matter when I received an extraordinary letter. It appeared to be sent by an acquaintance of mine from the neighboring country, with whom I had been friends since my school days. It was an envelope of the kind he had been using for years. It had his handwriting on the front, and his name was printed on the back. The letter I removed from the envelope, however, had nothing to do with me or him: it was addressed to a certain Oswald Schulte and signed by one Trude Danzig, two people whose existence I hadn't been aware of until that very moment. I immediately recalled Bogelin's hint. The letters must have gotten switched at the agency responsible for the surveillance of the mail. In other words, I now had conclusive evidence that I was under observation.

It is well known that in moments of distress one is more inclined to commit heedless acts, and I was no exception. As soon as I had finished reading the letter, I picked up the phone book, found Oswald Schulte's number, and called him. When he answered, I asked him if he knew Trude Danzig. In light of the letter, this was an utterly redundant question, but in my panicked state I asked it anyway. Mr. Schulte replied that, yes, Miss Danzig was well known to him, and he inquired whether I had a message from her. I was about to explain the peculiar circumstances that brought us together, when I realized the immense stupidity of what I was doing. I hung up the phone and sat there in despair. I told myself, although far too late, that it is only logical that the phones of those whose mail is monitored would be monitored as well. In the eyes of the agency, one suspect was now in relation to another. To make matters worse, I had ended the conversation before mentioning the mix-up in letters. Of course, I could have called Oswald Schulte a second time and explained the situation to him. To the ears of those listening in, however, this would have sounded like an attempt to cover myself, and in a manner that could have been interpreted as defaming the agency. Apart

from that, I was repulsed by the idea of explaining anything to this Mr. Schulte, who in all likelihood would
have been under surveillance for a reason.

For a long time I sat without moving to avoid acting
hastily again, and then I devised a plan. I told myself
that a false starting point creates its own logic, that all
of a sudden a consequentiality comes into existence that
seems imperative to those who are acting in error. The
suspicion I was under was such a false starting point,
and every one of my usual actions, which under normal circumstances would seem harmless and without
significance to the agency, would serve to confirm and
reinforce it over and over. Thus, in order to invalidate
the suspicion, I just had to do nothing and say nothing
for a sufficient amount of time, and it would necessar-
ily be dismissed due to a lack of sustenance. I trusted
myself to do this, being somebody who prefers listening
to speaking and standing still to walking. Finally, I said
to myself that my rescue shouldn't be long in coming,
that it need not wait if I was true to myself.

The first step I took was to break up with my girlfriend, who potentially could have been a bad girlfriend
for me in the eyes of the agency. For a short time, I
entertained the idea that she might be a member of the
surveillance team. She had unrestricted insight into all
my dealings. However, I found no evidence for this and
parted from her without any such suspicions. I don't
want to claim that the separation didn't affect me at

all, but it wasn't a big deal either. I seized on the very first pretense, puffed it up a little, and two days later everything that belonged to her was gone from my apartment. I felt lonely the first night after her departure, the next two nights I didn't sleep well, and after that I was over her.

At my office I faked an ailment of the vocal chords, which—so I claimed repeatedly in a croaking voice—hurt me whenever I spoke. As a result, no one noticed that I stopped talking. My colleagues' conversations began to steer clear of me, which soon became so natural that I didn't need the vocal chord excuse anymore. I was happy to see that, with time, I was being noticed less and less. During lunch breaks, I stopped going to the canteen and started bringing a lunch from home, which I would eat at my desk. I made an effort to appear constantly like someone who was busy thinking and didn't wish to be disturbed while doing so. I also considered becoming a careless employee instead of a good one. I decided, however, that conscientious work, as had always come naturally to me, couldn't possibly have been the reason for the suspicions against me, that if anything carelessness would be a reason to keep an eye on me. Thus, the only one of my habits that remained unchanged was that I completed my work in a timely and diligent fashion.

Once, while in the bathroom, I overheard two colleagues talking about me. It was like a final flare-up of interest in my affairs. One of them expressed the belief that I must be afflicted by some sorrow, that I had lost my old vitality. The other one said: Sometimes it just happens that a person doesn't feel like being sociable. The first one replied that maybe they should pay me some attention, maybe I was in a situation where I could use consoling. The other one ended the conversation by asking: Is it really any of our business, though?—for which I was very grateful to him.

I was already determined to disconnect my phone and yet refrained from doing so: it could have created the impression that I was trying to remove a means of observation. Nevertheless, I stopped using the phone. There was nobody I needed to call, and whenever it rang I wouldn't pick up the handset. After a few weeks, people stopped calling me—I had elegantly solved the telephone problem. For a short while, I wondered whether it wasn't suspicious for the owner of a phone never to make any calls. I answered myself that I would have to decide between an assumption and its opposite. I couldn't hold both to be equally suspicious. Otherwise, all that remained for me was to go insane.

I changed my behavior wherever I could discern regular habits. To achieve this, I studied myself with great patience. Some of the changes seemed exaggerated; some made me feel ridiculous. I made them anyway, telling myself: What do I know about how a suspicion evolves? I bought a gray suit, even though

I like bright and vibrant colors. I was convinced that what I liked mattered least now. Unless it was of vital importance, I didn't leave the house anymore. I stopped paying the rent in advance and in cash to my landlord, but instead paid by money order. An overdue notice—I had never received one before—conveniently followed. Some days I would take the train to work, some days I would walk the long way. One morning a schoolchild approached me and wanted to know the time. I held my watch out to him. The next day I left it at home. I contemplated to the point of exhaustion which aspects of my behavior were habitual and which were coincidental. Often, I couldn't answer the question, and in those cases I decided in favor of habit.

It would be wrong to believe that I felt unobserved in my apartment. Again, I thought: What do I know? I threw out all books and magazines that might reflect negatively on their owner. At first, I was certain that such writings weren't to be found in my possession anyway. Soon, however, I was surprised by what kind of material had made its way into my apartment. From time to time, I would switch on the radio or television, but only to watch programs that I wouldn't have watched before. Not surprisingly, I didn't enjoy these programs, and so this problem was solved as well. During the first weeks I often stood by the window to watch what little was happening outside. Soon, however, I began to consider whether someone who stands by the window for hours might not seem like a person keeping watch. I pulled down the blinds and accepted the possibility that it might appear as though I was trying to hide something, or hide myself.

Life in the apartment continued by lamplight, but as it stood I hardly needed light anyway. When I came home from the office, I ate a little, then lay down and thought for a while, if I felt like it. If not, I would doze until I achieved a comfortably mellow state, which was difficult to distinguish from sleep. Then I would really sleep, until the alarm clock woke me in the morning, and so on. Sometimes during those days I would be annoyed by my dreams. They were oddly wild and scattered and bore no relation to my life. I was a little ashamed about this and thought it very convenient that I couldn't be observed in my dreams as well. But then I thought: What do I know? I thought: How quickly a word slips from the mouth of someone sleeping, a word that might come as a revelation to an observer. In my situation, I would have considered it reckless to assume that I wouldn't be held responsible for my dreams to the extent anyone was aware of their nature. So I attempted to get rid of them, in which I succeeded with astonishing ease. I can't really say how this success came about. The quiet and uneventfulness of my days certainly helped as much as my resolve to be rid of my dreams. In any case, soon my sleep resembled a kind of death, and when the ringing of the alarm woke me in the morning, I rose to life from a black hole.

Now and then I couldn't avoid exchanging a few words with someone while shopping or at the office. The words appeared superfluous to me, but I had to say them in order not to appear rude. I used my best efforts to avoid having to be asked questions. If I was nevertheless forced to speak, my own words droned in my ears, and my tongue balked at the abuse.

Soon I had gotten used to not looking at people anymore. By virtue of this, I spared myself many an unpleasant view. I concentrated on matters that were actually important. It is well known how easily people mistake a gaze into their eyes for an invitation to converse—I had now ruled out this possibility. I watched where I was going, I looked for whatever I had to grab onto or avoid. At home I hardly made use of my eyes anymore at all. It soon seemed as though I had begun to move about more securely, and only rarely would I stumble anymore. After this experience, I would venture to say that the lowered view is the natural one. What use is it, I asked myself, when one is always proudly raising one's gaze and constantly blundering as a consequence? I also spared myself from noticing the way others looked at me, whether amiably, spitefully, compassionately, or with contempt. I no longer needed to take it into account. I hardly knew who I was dealing with anymore, and this contributed more than a little to my inner peace.

So, a year went by. I hadn't set a term for this lifestyle, but now, after quite a long while, I felt a wish that it might soon be enough. I felt I was at a crossroads, that I was slowly losing the ability to just live for the moment. If that was what I really wanted, I told myself, then fine, I could continue existing this way in the future. If not, it had to end now. Still, the longing I suddenly felt for the old times seemed childish and even illogical to me, and yet it was strong. I thought it likely that the suspicion brought against me was long gone. There was no other reasonable possibility.

On a Monday night, I decided to go out. I stood in my darkened living room and didn't feel like sleeping or dozing. I raised the blinds, not a little but all the way, then I turned on the light. Then I took money from a drawer—I would like to mention that all of a sudden I had plenty of money, because throughout the year I had earned normally but spent only very little. So I put the money in my pocket and didn't quite know what for. I thought, A beer might not be a bad idea right now.

My heart began to beat like it hadn't in ages when I stepped out into the street. I began to walk, without knowing where to exactly. My favorite bar didn't exist anymore; I knew this. I planned to enter the first bar that appealed to me. I realized this would most likely be the first bar along the way. I planned not to take on too much for the first night: have a beer, look at a few people, listen to them. To speak myself would have seemed premature. There would be more than enough opportunity for that in the future. Yet, when I reached the first bar, I couldn't bring myself to open the door. I felt childish, and yet I had to walk on: suddenly, I was afraid that once I opened the door, all the patrons would stare at me. After a few steps, I promised myself not to give in to such a silly fear again. Out of pure coincidence, I turned around and noticed a man following me.

At first, I could only assume he was following me, of course. After a few minutes, however, I was sure, because I had made the stupidest detours without shaking him. He stayed behind me at the very same distance even when I ran a little. It seemed like he didn't care whether I noticed him or not. I don't want to say I felt threatened exactly, but nevertheless I was gripped by horror. I thought: Nothing is over after a whole year! I'm still presumed to be an endangerer. How am I doing it? Then I thought: Worst of all, my behavior didn't even seem to matter. The suspicion had taken on a life of its own. It may have had to do with me, but I certainly had nothing to do with it. This is what I thought as I walked ahead of the man.

When I got home, I pulled the blinds back down. I lay in bed to ponder my future. I had already begun to resolve to live this way for a second year. Then I told myself: Surely the security of the state can only be maintained if its protectors miss the mark from time to time. That's exactly what had happened in my case and was still happening. In the end, being under surveillance hadn't really hurt me. The past year hadn't been forced on me, I thought. I didn't need to go looking for a culprit: I had prescribed it myself.

Then I fell asleep, full of impatience. I awoke before my alarm rang and couldn't wait to look the first person to greet me in the eye and reply, "Good morning," regardless of what might come of it.

Translated by Jonathan Becker

Romeo

The greatest difficulty for me is the language. German is like the enemy's forest: you dodge one trap and you've already stepped into the next one. If it weren't for that cursed language, I wouldn't feel so much contempt. I look like someone who could be from anywhere, and whenever I have a meal with garlic in it I rinse my mouth out thoroughly. I would smash some of their faces in if I knew a better way to earn money. In five years, I'll have earned enough unless tragedy strikes. The man at the bank treats me as if I'd stolen the money I'm depositing from *him*. He taps his finger repeatedly on the spot where I'm supposed to sign and looks at me with impatience. I hope that, in five years when I withdraw it all, it will be the same man. I'll put the whole amount in my pocket and tell him not to look at me like it was his money. He'll shrug his shoulders disparagingly and tell me with his eyes that I'm scum. Next I'll tell him to take his ugly eyes off me. Maybe I'll say he can look at his wife that way, if she'll put up with it, but not me. Then he'll ask whether I've gone crazy. One way or another he'll insult me, my witnesses will hear it, and then he'll be in for a surprise.

I didn't choose this city, at least not in the sense that I weighed the advantages and disadvantages. When it was finally my turn at the office, I was offered the choice between this one and another city I'd never heard of before. So I decided for Berlin, but it didn't mean much to me. Only since living here have I realized how convenient this place is for someone who wants to save money. I didn't realize it at the beginning, but gradually, and surprisingly late. In the first month, the only exchange rate I cared about was the one between my own currency and the money I'm earning here. I had been planning to go to East Berlin sometime anyway, to cure the boredom on a warm Sunday, partly because you're supposed to take an interest in the sights of the city you live in. It was then I heard from a Greek coworker that one currency could be exchanged for the other at a very favorable rate. He wondered how it was I didn't know about this already. He explained which things are expensive over here and which are expensive over there. Soon I understood that, if one just goes about it the right way, it's possible to increase one's earnings significantly. He did say that exchanging money is prohibited in the other Berlin, and the punishment if they catch you is quite severe. But he also said only a millionaire could afford to respect that.

So I began to inform myself, mostly asking people from my home country. I wanted to hear about the experiences of many people, to pick the best and avoid rookie mistakes. The most reasonable thing appeared to be to do as many would have liked but only few dared: to stay in the other Berlin and actually live there, and only work in this one for the better money. I calculated that, if I tried this, I could shorten my five years abroad to only three and a half. To four at the very most, and where else are you given a free year?

My limited experience at the border told me that the guards are very rude but not very thorough. I met a kindhearted fellow countryman who had been living like this for a long time, and he provided me with information unreservedly. He said you have to meet a girl with a large room, since you're not allowed to have your own room. To find someone with two rooms, he said, would be immensely lucky, almost no one has two rooms. To find a nice girl, however, isn't too hard, he said, at least not as hard as it is here, because you can bring her a thousand things that you can't buy there. One inconvenience is that you have to leave the other Berlin at midnight, that's the law. But you can turn around on the other side of the border and go straight back. This way, you cross the border four times in one day: once in the morning on your way to work, the second time after work, then just before twelve because of the damned law, and one last time after twelve, back to the girl. Except for weekends of course, when there is no commute. Another possibility, he said, is to hang around town until midnight and then go to the girl and get into bed. It depends on whether the girl is willing to play along and whether you can handle it yourself, physically. In this way you can save at least eleven marks fifty in one day, that's the fee for crossing the border. He said, because of this he can send his wife an extra two hundred marks every month.

When, soon after, the already expensive rent for my room was raised by an inordinate amount, I was ready. The next Saturday I crossed the border and went to a bar that had been recommended to me for my purposes. At first, I was disappointed, because looking around I couldn't seem to spot what I was looking for. Instead, I heard the men sitting at the table next to mine speak in my language. Five minutes later we were sitting together, telling stories about our villages. One of them was from a place over the mountains that I'd heard of before. After a few glasses, two women arrived who were meeting the men. They all left together, but one of the women came back and asked me if I wanted her to bring along her friend next Saturday. Because I was unprepared and embarrassed, I acted like an idiot and said I didn't even know her friend. To my relief, she wasn't offended and said: I expected that, it's why I wanted to bring her. And she also said: Looking is free. We set a time for next Saturday. One of my fellow countrymen winked at me from the door, as if he was behind the whole thing. Actually, I was happy to have made the first step without much effort.

My head was spinning a little after the three or four glasses of wine I'd had. When I thought about the exchange rate between the two currencies, food and drink were unbelievably cheap here. I would have been able to afford much more wine, liquor even, but it was still early in the day. I didn't feel like going back, there was nothing waiting for me. I wanted to go see a movie. I could do that here just as well as in West Berlin, only much cheaper. I waited a long time for the waiter, when a woman sat down at my table. I saw that all the other tables were full. The first thing I noticed was her fingernails, which were the same color as the unripe plums in our garden. She took a very long cigarette from a new pack and I gave her a light. She had a way of looking at you that seemed a bit bold to me. When the waiter finally arrived, I ordered coffee instead of paying. I might have done that even without the woman. She asked me where I was from, and I told her. As I was speaking, I noticed she was older than I had first thought. In fact, she was probably forty. She said I didn't even look like a foreigner. It was obvious she was trying to flatter me. I enjoyed that. For the first time in my life, I felt like a rich man. I don't mean someone who can afford a lot of things, more like someone held in esteem. She had cake with whipped cream and told me that on the weekends she usually took a boat out on one of the rivers, that there wasn't much going on in the city. Then she talked about a television series I didn't know; I don't even own a television. She had taken off one of her shoes. It was lying next to her chair, almost out in the aisle.

A little later I began to consider whether I should invite her to the movies. She would have joined me—I have an eye for these things—but something held me back. It wasn't her age, more her demeanor. I can't really express it in words. I was looking for someone with a room, after all, but I didn't want to live with *her*. If I hadn't had any other opportunities, I might not have been so picky. But I had the prospect of the coming Saturday, and I could hope I would like the other woman's friend better. So I spent a few more minutes listening to her mouth, which wouldn't stop talking, then I told her I had an appointment and had to leave now. The woman's eyes stayed friendly, as they had been the entire time, but she immediately stopped talking. In a way I felt sorry for her, but I told myself I better reserve my pity for me. Until I had settled the check with the waiter, she had the expression of someone trying to figure out a difficult problem. Then I said goodbye. She even shook my hand and said: Have fun. I went outside and wished I had a nice car I could drive around in.

The next Saturday, I couldn't find a free table at the restaurant. Because the weather was so bad, they all wanted to sit inside and drink coffee, and I had to wait at the door. A waiter told me I couldn't stand in the aisle. Had I stepped outside, I would have gotten wet. He kept saying it to me until I turned up my collar and stepped outdoors. At home he wouldn't have been able to do that. I'm very strong. Through the window, I could see he was just as rude to his fellow Germans, and I couldn't understand why they put up with it.

After a while, the two women arrived, way too late. I immediately recognized the first one: she was wearing the same jacket she had worn a week ago. The other one, the one I was expecting, was neither pretty nor ugly. There was nothing remarkable about her at all, so all I was able to ascertain was that she was a young woman or a girl. She seemed a little shy. I liked that. The one in the green jacket gave her a nudge, then she introduced me to her friend: Klara. Then she looked at her watch, acted as if it was very late for her, and left. I was happy that it wasn't her I had waited for. I remembered her saying: Looking is free.

I said to Klara that there weren't any free tables at this restaurant and asked whether she had any alternative suggestions. She shrugged her shoulders. Since it wouldn't stop raining, though, we couldn't stay out there. I asked her again for a dry place nearby. I hoped, of course, that she had her own apartment and would invite me there. She thought about it for a moment and named another restaurant and said we should be able to get a table there. While we walked there, I was relieved in a way that we weren't going to her apartment. If it was going to work out between us, I thought, it was probably for the better. I just hoped that the reason she wasn't taking me to her apartment was not that she didn't have one.

At the other restaurant, we were almost the only patrons. As we studied the menu, I said she didn't have to look at the prices. She ordered chocolate ice cream with egg liqueur and I had wine. She was a nurse, like her friend. It took quite a while for her to stop being ashamed when she talked. Until then, I had to pull every word out of her, despite struggling with my own inhibitions. I wondered whether it had been her own wish to meet someone like me, or whether her friend had decided it for her. The friend didn't really seem to fit with her. Suddenly, I found her mouth pretty and felt like kissing her. I imagined our getting together had nothing to do with this or the other Berlin and nothing to do with the two currencies. I imagined I was simply a young man and she the girl that came with that. I told her a dirty joke and she smiled a little.

When it stopped raining, we walked around for a while. The streets were empty. She said surely there was more going on at this hour on our side of the border. I replied that her assumption was correct, but I actually didn't mind the quiet. She said: Strange. We checked an advertising column, but there were no movies she wanted to see. She seemed halfhearted in everything she said or did. She reminded me of my little brother, the way he poked around in his soup, not because he didn't like the soup but because he didn't like to eat at all. He became thin like a stick because of it. But I didn't know her yet, and it was possible she just happened to be in that kind of mood today.

My right foot was hurting—an electric cart had run over it two days earlier on the factory floor. It wasn't only the driver's fault. I had been careless, too. I couldn't spend the entire day walking around. Besides, that wasn't what I was here for. I asked what she normally did with her free time, especially on the weekends. She told me all the boring things that make up weekends everywhere: cleaning, meeting girlfriends, television, visiting parents. I inquired whether she had a boyfriend. I said: A pretty girl like you would surely have a boyfriend. She became shy again and went silent for a whole block. Then she told me she had had a few boyfriends, but only two serious ones. The first one had suddenly broken up with her, she still had no idea why, and the second one she had sent away, because he wasn't treating her well enough. She said: Besides, I'm not pretty at all. I considered whether I would have preferred meeting a girl who was more like a whore, like her friend, for example. I saw a few advantages and a few disadvantages either way. Then I told myself that such comparisons of women are foolish to begin with. There is always something better.

Suddenly she said: If you want, we can go to my place. It sounded as if it wasn't her idea but a piece of advice someone had given her that she just now remembered. I was quite surprised and said: Why not? She said she didn't have anything at home except for tomato juice, in case I wanted to drink wine or liquor. I put my arm around her shoulder as we walked: she wasn't supposed to get the impression I was indifferent to her offer. I said it couldn't hurt to buy some wine and I very much liked her idea. She said that for someone who has only been here for such a short time my German was very good.

She took me to the only store open at this hour on a Saturday. Unlike the streets outside, it was busy. We bought two bottles of wine and white chocolate, but I couldn't pay with the money I'd changed that was sitting in my pocket. I was told they only accepted the other money here, which was a shame. Klara looked at blouses in a shop display. When I asked whether she'd like one, she shook her head and walked out ahead of me. Her apartment was far away. We had to take the subway and then countless stops on the bus. She linked arms with me as we were sitting next to each other on the bus. I wondered whether the distance from the border crossing didn't make the entire exercise pointless. But then the house appeared in a green suburban street.

She spent a long time looking for her keys. In the window next to the entrance sat a red dog that was yawning. The apartment was big enough for two, I realized after a few minutes. She had a large room, a toilet, and a kitchen that was good for washing. Above the stove, some panties and stockings were hung on a clothesline. She removed them quickly and hid them as if they were a disgrace. She placed the two wine bottles in the sink and ran cold water over them.

As soon as we sat down on the couch, I held her and kissed her. I knew I'd become shy if I waited too long. I remembered from before. At first she remained still, but then she opened her mouth and began kissing back, and I thought, there's that out of the way. I could touch her wherever I wanted, without her putting up any resistance. We didn't even have that much time: it was long past seven, I had to be at the border by twelve, and there were lots of stations between here and there. I went to the kitchen, dried off a wine bottle, and looked for some glasses. I was glad she didn't follow me. It was like an invitation to move about freely in her apartment. When I returned to the room with the wine and glasses, she had drawn the curtains and turned on the television. She said the programs on Saturday nights were always good.

We drank and ate the white chocolate. She was so immersed in the television images there was no talking to her, even though it was mostly singing. I could only pick out single words, my German isn't good enough for songs, and a lot of the singing was also in English. After a while she asked me whether I could bring back a certain record for her. This was the first sign that she had plans for me, too. I let her write the name down on a piece of paper for me. To do that she turned on the light for a moment. I drank much more wine than she did. It annoyed me how important the television was to her, but I didn't want to start setting rules on the first night, acting like the man of the house. I lay behind her on the sofa. The shadows of the figures in the television were dancing on the ceiling. Klara's fingers were lying directly in front of my eyes and were moving tirelessly with the music. Only when there was talking did they stop.

I took the money I'd changed from my pocket and put it on the table. It was still in the envelope from the bank. I didn't want to carry it back across the border and back again the next time I came over. It had been burning a hole in my pocket the whole time during the border control. Of course, I could hardly ask Klara for a receipt, but we didn't know each other well enough yet for the money. I resolved to wait for the rest of the evening and then decide whether I could leave the envelope or not. I told myself: If she watches television the entire time, I'll be none the wiser.

I pulled her down to me by her hair. She didn't resist and said: I guess you're right. We kissed. Suddenly, she didn't seem shy at all. Not because she was kissing me so passionately or skillfully, but more that she was kissing me in a somewhat detached way, almost like it was a matter of course. I wondered why she didn't want me to buy the blouse for her at the store earlier. I would have liked to turn off the television: it interrupts you because you keep understanding a few words here and there or because you're trying to remember who the singer reminds you of. But when my hand reached for the switch, Klara pulled it back. I had never made love with the television running, not least because I didn't own one. She said: Leave it, it's fine. I once had a thing with a girl who wound her watch in the middle of sex. I got my revenge on her, but I don't want to say how.

We kissed again for a little while, then we got undressed. First I undressed her, then she undressed me. I tried to hold her in such a way that she couldn't see the television. We began to make love, but I already knew it wouldn't be anything special. Her eyes were closed, and she held me without moving, as if that was a rule. Because she was a nurse, I didn't need to ask her any questions. I like when girls move and make some noise, when they show you there's something going on with them and you're not having fun all by yourself. She lay impossibly still, and only her mouth, when we kissed or when she licked her lips, showed me she hadn't fallen asleep. I tried all sorts of things, I explored her body—which all of a sudden seemed tiny to me—for any sensitive spots. I had once learned in a sex education movie that everyone has these spots, you just have to find them. But I couldn't find them.

A new program started on the television. Maybe she was listening intently and wasn't thinking about us at all. I thought I could probably risk leaving the money, she didn't seem like she would cheat me out of it. Then I couldn't wait any longer, and the lovemaking had to come to an end. I leaned close to her ear and asked her whether she had finished, too. She said: A while ago. I resolved to deal with this issue later, if we stayed together. I told her: If you show you're having fun more, you'll have more fun. But she didn't react. She drank a little wine, then she said that every three weeks she had to work the night shift. It was the second clear sign that she had plans for me. I would have wished for a better sign, but at least I now knew that I could leave the money. It seemed too early to be talking about living arrangements on this first night.

I fell asleep and dreamed of home, as I do almost every night. I woke up and was shocked, but Klara immediately said there was still enough time. She wondered about the money on the table, which she had discovered in the meantime, and I explained it to her. I said I wanted to leave it here until next time, because it would be stupid to carry forbidden money back and forth across the border. I acted as though we had already agreed on our next meeting, and she didn't seem to mind. She stood up, took the envelope with the money and put it in a drawer with her underwear. She asked whether I knew exactly how much it was. I said yes, because naturally I knew exactly how much it was, it was a stupid question. She came back to the couch and stroked my chest, which surprised me, and we made love again. She had completely changed, as if the first time she had just been practicing and only now was getting serious. I thought how mysterious love is. She looked at me now and moved her arms and used her hands, and I liked her a hundred times better. I asked what was going on all of a sudden, and she said: What do you mean? As if she didn't even know what I was talking about.

Later, she went to the kitchen to make some sandwiches. I was happy, because it was quite nice with her and I could just as well have ended up with someone else. Of course, I wouldn't have had to end up with just anyone, I know that. But when you're desperately trying to save money, you can't be too picky, and most of all you can't wait forever. I shouted to the kitchen, asking whether there was anything I could do to help. She laughed a little and shouted back that I should just stay put and relax. I liked that, too.

As I was getting dressed, I saw some numbers on the television; it was running the entire time. They looked like lottery numbers, and when Klara returned with the sandwiches, I asked whether there was a lottery in East Berlin. She said: Of course there's a lottery. I enjoyed the sandwiches. The slices of meat were cut very thick. She had brought the tomato juice, but I preferred to have some more wine. I told her that I play the lottery regularly every week in West Berlin, for four marks. I always play the same numbers and in the first week right away won five marks, but nothing since then. She did some calculations in her head then she said, four marks every week, that's more than two hundred marks a year. She asked whether there wasn't anything better I could be spending that kind of money on.

I explained to her that there's nothing better to spend four marks a week on. I don't need to be told that the chances of becoming a rich man by playing the lottery are small. But if I didn't play, the chances would be even smaller, and that hope is worth four marks a week to me. I told Klara about my mother, who has a similar habit—she just doesn't play the lottery. She gives the same amount of money to the church every month, not for a happy afterlife, I know that much, but because she's expecting some kind of miracle in this life. A few times she has encouraged me to do the same, but I consider her method pointless. Because if you could bribe God with four marks a week, he wouldn't be any good in the first place. When I play the lottery, I can become a millionaire for the same money.

Klara thought this was nonsense. She said: After all, it's your money you're throwing out the window. There wasn't much time left, and I didn't want to attract any attention on my first trip by being too late. I asked whether there was anything else she wanted me to get for her besides the record. She said nothing came to mind at the moment, but she could think about it until next time. She asked whether I wanted to come back the following Saturday, and I said yes, next Saturday. We have a proverb that goes: If you want your ox to pull your plow a little longer, you'll have to wait a little longer for its leather.

She told me she had to work the weekend after next. I said: It's a while until then. She sat next to me in her underwear. I could have made love to her again right then, but I didn't even kiss her. She had the bus timetable in her head. She said that to be safe I shouldn't wait for the very last one, because sometimes the bus was canceled. As she got dressed for the walk to the bus stop, I had a really good idea. I asked her for a piece of paper and wrote down all the numbers I played in the other lottery. I told her to mark these same numbers on a lottery ticket and play them for me every week from now on. I didn't know how much a lottery ticket was over here. Klara said about fifty pfennig, but she didn't know exactly. In any case the price was minute at this exchange rate. I was pleased with my idea. Of course, the same exchange rate applied to the winnings, but a quarter of the grand prize is still a grand prize. I told her to make sure to remember it every week, in case I ever forgot to mention it. She was welcome to think this was crazy, if only she didn't forget to buy the tickets. I was so excited at this new prospect that I drank the rest of the wine from the bottle. On the television they were now showing soccer. I would have liked to watch it, but we had to go.

There were a few people waiting at the bus stop; the last bus hadn't come. Klara said that was a good sign. They never canceled two buses in a row. We walked a few steps away from the bus stop so we could talk better. Again, she explained the way to the border in detail. Then she said she had remembered something I could get for her. She wanted a certain kind of hair spray, and I promised I would find it. She said the hair spray you could buy over here was so terribly sticky and didn't smell very nice either. I said she didn't have to explain herself: if she wanted something, I would just get it for her. Then we walked up and down a little bit because it was too chilly to stay in one spot. When the bus came around the corner, I reminded her again about the lottery tickets. She hugged me and asked quietly whether I really liked her. I said: Yes.

Translated by Jonathan Becker

The Invisible City

When I was two years old I came to this ghetto. At age five, I left it again, headed for the camp. I don't remember a thing. This is what people told me, this is what is in my papers, and this was, therefore, my childhood. Sometimes I think: What a shame that something else isn't written there. At any rate, I know the ghetto only from meager hearsay.

My father talked to me about it a few times, reluctantly and seldom. During his lifetime I wasn't curious enough to outsmart him with subtle questions, and then it was too late. Nevertheless, I wrote stories about the ghettos as if I were an expert. Perhaps I thought that if I could only write long enough, the memories would come. Perhaps at some point I even began to take some of my inventions for memories. Without memories of childhood, it's as if you're condemned to constantly carry around with you a box whose contents you don't know. And the older you get, the heavier the box feels and the more impatient you become to finally open it.

Now the floor of my room is littered with the photos of this exhibition. If I had memories, they would have to be at home there, on those streets, behind those walls, among these people. The women in the pictures interest me most: I don't know what my mother looked like. No photos of her exist. She died in the camp. I could just choose one of the women, I suppose. My father said that she was strikingly pretty, of course.

Most of the pictures convey a tranquillity for which we yearn. They radiate peacefulness. In my eyes, they depict something of *the good old days*. The photographer seems to have been striving to prove that the ghetto wasn't as gruesome a place as enemy propaganda might have insinuated, that things happened there as they do among the rest of humanity. Even though these people were a bit peculiar, a bit different. But we knew that before. If we look closely, we might even think that the ghetto was a place of meditation.

The young Jewish policeman, who examines the paperwork of a suspicious-looking passerby, as is the duty of police officers all over the world. The barber, who has taken off his cap before the photographer and waits for customers in front of his wooden house, which is certainly comfortable on the inside. The bearded man, who pulls a wagon with rubber tires over the cobblestones. The worker, who isn't exactly killing himself. Even the four Jews who carry a dead person alongside a wall don't deserve more than a brief moment of pity. For four people, carrying a corpse can't be all that hard, and death happens everywhere. We might actually have more sympathy for the German guard next to the sentry box, standing there so far from home and so lost. It's so damn lonely at the entrance to the ghetto. No one wants to go in and no one out. The pictures suggest that everything is carefully regulated here, in a manner deeply inherent to the things and people.

In short, I think up theories about the photographer's objectives. I see through his intentions; the guy can't fool me. But all of a sudden, something unsettling happens. Individual pictures absorb my gaze. I fall into them, far from any intention to write a text. I see two pictures of children. In the first, they wait for rations to be handed out, pots and little buckets and spoons in hand. In the second, they're wearing red caps and staring at the photographer. Interrupted at play and nonetheless motionless. No, a child as small as I must have been then is not to be seen. But there are probably children in the pictures who knew me, who took things away from me, or beat me up or ordered me around. Perhaps there is someone standing there who would be my best friend today, had things taken a slightly more favorable course.

I hate sentimentalities. They cloud the mind. I'd prefer to close up all the holes they might crawl out of. Each time my father was overcome by emotion, I left the room until he got hold of himself again. Suddenly, that's irrelevant. The pictures fill me with emotion, me of all people, and I have to wipe the most ridiculous tears from my eyes. No girls in the photos, just boys, boys, and more boys. Why is that? Is that the reason girls, for as far back as I can remember, have always been special creatures to me?

In one of the pictures, Jewish firefighters drive through the ghetto. What was it about those firefighters? My father told me something, that they existed, that he knew one of them, or that they always came too late, or that there was always something burning. I have forgotten even that. Constantly, I have the feeling that I simply need to make a bit more of an effort to remember, instead of waiting lazily and lethargically for the memories to come to me. But I make an effort until I go crazy, and nothing comes. Only the pictures lie in my room, so incomprehensibly near.

When I received them, when I opened the package and began to spread them out, I soon had the sense that I needed to put them in a different order. But, in what kind of an order? What belonged to what and what should be separated? Do children belong with children and bearded men with bearded men and tradesmen with tradesmen? And police officers with police officers and blondes with blondes? In any case, the order isn't right. It's like a crack in a disk that ruins the most beautiful record. I order and reorder the pictures over and over again. I want to solve the puzzle. I put the train station on the outside, the cemetery on the outside, the streets in the center, wooden houses together, stone houses together, the workshops in between, the border on the border. Again and again everything is wrong. The little lamp of memory fails to light.

I stare at the pictures and search for that one decisive piece of my life until my eyes are sore, but only the vanishing lives of the others are recognizable. To what end should I speak of outrage or sympathy? I want to climb down among them and don't find the way.

Translated by Martin Bäumel and Tracy Graves

Acknowledgments

"The Wall" was originally published under the title "Die Mauer" in *Nach der ersten Zukunft*, Suhrkamp Verlag, 1980.

"The Tale of the Sick Princess" is taken from Jurek Becker's novel *Jacob the Liar*, translated into English by Leila Vennewitz, published by Arcade Publishing.

"The Most Popular Family Story" was originally published under the title "Die beliebteste Familiengeschichte" in *Nach der ersten Zukunft*, Suhrkamp Verlag, 1980.

"The Suspect" was originally published under the title "Der Verdächtige" in *Nach der ersten Zukunft*, Suhrkamp Verlag, 1980.

"Romeo" was originally published under the same title in: *Nach der ersten Zukunft*, Suhrkamp Verlag, 1980.

"The Invisible City" appeared in the catalog accompanying the exhibition *Unser einziger Weg ist Arbeit* (Our Only Chance Is to Work), 1990, and was collected in *Ende des Grössenwahns*, published by Suhrkamp Verlag, 1996. This translation first appeared in *My Father, the Germans and I*, by Jurek Becker, published by Seagull Books in 2010, and is reprinted here by the kind permission of the publishers.